"Follow
the sparrow
to the
Mad King's
castle."

CAHILLS vs. VESPERS

A KING'S RANSOM

THE **39** CLUES

JUDE WATSON

SCHOLASTIC INC.

NEW YORK TORONTO LONDON AUCKLAND
SYDNEY MEXICO CITY NEW DELHI HONG KONG

For Albert Blundell,
who loved words
and raised a writer.
—J.W.

All rights reserved. Published by
Scholastic Inc., *Publishers since 1920.*
SCHOLASTIC, THE 39 CLUES, and associated logos
are trademarks and/or registered trademarks of Scholastic Inc.

Library of Congress Control Number: 2011930647

ISBN: 978-0-545-32410-6
10 9 8 7 6 5 4 3 2 1   11 12 13 14 15

Book design by SJI Associates, Inc.
bones p. 130: CG Textures
hostages p. 136: Ken Karp for Scholastic
De Virga Map p. 158: Wikimedia Commons
All other images created for Scholastic by Keirsten Geise,
Charice Silverman, and Rainne Wu.
Library edition, December 2011
Printed in China   62

Scholastic US: 557 Broadway • New York, NY 10012
Scholastic Canada: 604 King Street West • Toronto, ON M5V 1E1
Scholastic New Zealand Limited: Private Bag 94407 • Greenmount, Manukau 2141
Scholastic UK Ltd.: Euston House • 24 Eversholt Street • London NW1 1DB

CHAPTER 1

Florence, Italy

Dan Cahill didn't realize just how many policemen there were in the world until he became an international art thief.

At this early hour, the Santa Maria Novella train station was crammed with travelers. Businessmen with briefcases, students chugging espressos, tourists with too much luggage, and two teenagers, one with a stolen priceless thirteenth-century book in a backpack.

That would be him.

Dan hung his thumbs on the straps of his pack, hugging it closer to him. He almost felt that Marco Polo's original manuscript, *Il Milione* — the one that had been lost for centuries until he and his sister had found it hidden in the Colosseum in Rome — was actually emitting heat. Was that why he was sweating so badly?

Or was it the fact that there seemed to be a policeman every five feet?

"*Polizia* everywhere," his sister, Amy, murmured.

"They're checking passports at the boarding platforms," Dan noted. He watched as a uniformed officer stopped two young students about to board a train. They were older than he and Amy, but the girl had brown hair to her shoulders like Amy, and the boy was wiry like Dan.

At least he and his sister had fake passports and disguises. He couldn't get used to the sight of Amy in a blond wig, and his heavy framed glasses screamed *DORK*, or whatever that was in Italian. *Il Dorko?*

"What we need is a distraction," Amy murmured. "If they look at our passports too closely, we could be in trouble. We've got to get on that train to Switzerland!"

"Because when a deranged psycho gives you orders, it's important to snap to," Dan said.

The text had come only a few hours before.

Perhaps you notice that your loved ones continue to accept our Vesper hospitality. This is due to your previous treachery. They will remain our guests until you complete four more tasks. The first of these will be in Lucerne, Switzerland. I suggest you get yourselves there immediately, lest the number of our little party dwindles.

Vesper One

Their enemy Vesper One was a big fan of the mocking taunt. Every word was a thrust to the heart, letting them know that he was holding members of their family hostage and was prepared to kill them.

Dan stared up at the train departures board as if it would hold all the answers. Why was he here, desperate and scared, instead of back in Massachusetts, trying to scam himself out of math homework like any normal thirteen-year-old?

Wherever they turned, headlines screamed the news: *IL CRIMINE DEL SECOLO!* The crime of the century. They had stolen a Caravaggio from the Uffizi Gallery, and now they were on Interpol's most-wanted list. Which would have been sort of cool if he didn't have to be afraid of going to jail for ten thousand years.

Lives were on the line. Lives of people they had become close to, including Reagan Holt, Ted Starling, and Natalie Kabra. Twelve-year-old Phoenix Wizard. And people they loved — their Uncle Alistair Oh and their guardians, Fiske Cahill and Nellie Gomez. That was the hardest thing to bear. Fiske had disappeared in California, and Nellie had been kidnapped right off the streets of Paris.

The destinations on the board blurred, and Dan rocked on his feet with weariness. He heard the hiss of an espresso machine. Over his head the loudspeaker announced a track change in Italian and English. Everything seemed to fade a little. "I'm so beat I could lie down right on the floor," he told Amy. "When was the last time we slept?"

"Day before yesterday?" Amy asked with a frown. "I know what you mean. This is some jet lag. Let's get a coffee while we make a plan."

"Oh, yeah, jet lag. That must be it," Dan agreed as he trailed after her to the espresso bar. "Not the fact that we pulled off a museum heist, went without sleep and food, and oh, yeah—did I mention this—almost got killed? Jet lag. *That's* why we're tired."

"Well, if you want to get *technical*," Amy said, but she summoned up a smile for her brother. She pushed balled-up paper money at the counterman and held up two fingers for coffee.

"I wonder what he wants us to steal next," Dan said. "I think I maxed out my museum heist skills."

"If we could just get one step ahead of them . . ." Amy murmured. She took the change from the counterman and handed an espresso to Dan.

He took a sip and his face turned red. He let out a series of explosive coughs, stamping his foot with each one. Passersby turned and stared, and Amy saw a policeman's gaze sweep the crowd, looking for the source of the commotion.

She grabbed the now-empty espresso cup and put it back on the counter, pushing Dan forward and quickly maneuvering him through the crowd.

"I said *distraction*," she hissed. "Not *pandemonium*."

"I couldn't help it," Dan wheezed. "Dude, what was that sludge I just inhaled?"

"Just Italian coffee," Amy said. "Look, the train to Lucerne leaves in fifteen minutes. We have to take a chance."

Dan scanned the crowd. "You know what we need? A—tuba!"

"A *what*?"

Dan pointed with his chin. Off to their right, a tuba seemed to be floating through the crowd. Dan began to follow it, with Amy trailing behind. Suddenly, it dropped out of sight. Amy and Dan skirted a family running for a train and saw a slender young woman slumped on a suitcase, holding a tuba and crying. A large sticker on a small trunk read WILMINGTON WOWZABELLES EUROPEAN TOUR.

"Distraction!" Dan crowed.

They moved forward, not knowing what they'd do or say but knowing they had the perfect opportunity for . . . something.

"Need a hand with that?" Dan asked the girl. "I happen to have experience as a tuba wrangler."

She looked up, startled. Her eyes were a warm brown behind her delicate wire-rimmed glasses. She smiled. "Thanks, but I think I have it covered." Dan detected a slight Southern accent. Suddenly, her eyes filled with tears. "Actually, I don't! I missed the train, and I have the tuba and all the costumes! It's all Heather's fault. She just had to get her last Italian gelato before the train. She *told* me to just watch the tuba for *two seconds* and she'd come back. If I don't make it to Zurich in time, I'm doomed!"

"Hey, we're going to Switzerland, too!" Dan said.

"You are?" She swiped at her tears. "I'll miss the concert. My suitcase is with Ms. Mutchnik, and my charger's in my bag, so I can't even call them. And I c-can't speak Italian!" she exclaimed, her eyes wide, as though this was the final awful thing that had happened.

"You can borrow my phone," Amy offered. "And you could take the train to Lucerne with us and then go to Zurich from there. We can travel together."

"Really? That would be so awesome! Europe kind of freaks me out, y'all, to tell you the truth," the girl confided, leaning toward them. "I've never traveled much." Awkwardly, the girl struggled to her feet. She stuck out her hand. "Vanessa Mallory, from Wilmington, South Carolina."

"Mark Farley," Dan said, remembering the name on his fake passport just in time. "This is my sister . . ." His mind was a blank.

"Caroline," Amy supplied. "But you can call me Carrie! We're from Maine," she improvised.

"It's so awesome that I bumped into you," Vanessa said, shouldering one of the bags.

They hurried to the track and got in line behind a wealthy-looking woman with a large trunk and several suitcases. She was dressed in a fur coat and hat, even though it wasn't that cold. She spoke sharply to the police officer at the train door in rapid Italian. He shrugged.

Finally, the line moved forward. Amy pulled the Wowzabelles trunk, and Dan grabbed the tuba.

"On your way to a concert?" The policeman smiled.

Vanessa nodded. "We're on a European tour," she added proudly.

"And what is a Wowzabelle?" he asked.

"Awesome singers," Amy said, handing over her passport.

Dan waited while the policeman scrutinized the photo, comparing it to Amy. Then he reached for Dan's.

It seemed to take long seconds before he handed back the document. He ticketed the trunk. "This will go in the oversize compartment — pick it up in Zurich. Welcome aboard."

Only Dan heard Amy's long sigh of relief as they boarded the train and found their seats, stowing the tuba overhead.

Dan glanced out the window. A man in a raincoat was talking to the friendly policeman. He had a nose like the beak of a raptor, and his dark hair looked as though he'd blow-dried it with an airplane propeller.

Dan looked away, checking out the station, but his gaze snapped back. He didn't know why, exactly. Maybe because the man wasn't showing the officer a ticket or a passport, he was just leaning in, talking to him. And all the while his gaze swept the station.

Detective, Dan thought, as the policeman pointed to the Lucerne train.

CHAPTER 2

The man scanned the windows as he walked alongside the train. Dan shrank back.

He nudged Amy and tilted his head.

"Can I use your phone, Carrie?" Vanessa asked Amy. "I really need to call Ms. Mutchnik."

Vanessa leaned forward for the phone, and Amy crashed back against the seat. Now shielded by Vanessa, she was able to watch the man as he moved, his gaze on the windows.

The train started with a lurch. They saw his face briefly as they slid past him. He started to run as he tried to catch up and jump aboard. Had he seen them? The train accelerated, and he was left behind on the track. Dan and Amy exchanged a relieved glance. He could have been just a guy who missed his train. But somehow Dan didn't think so.

"I'm perfectly *fine*," Vanessa was saying. "The Farleys are awesome—they're from Maine, which is, like, the nicest state *ever*. I have Heather's tuba, I have the costumes, and I even have a sandwich. No, you don't have to meet me at the station . . . oh, whatever. No! Don't call my parents! I am so incredibly *fine*. . . ."

As the city of Florence receded, Dan felt himself relax. He and Amy had learned during the hunt for the 39 Clues to grab rest when they could. He yawned. The slight sway of the train reminded him of his grandmother Grace's hammock on the lawn on a warm September afternoon, back when he had nobody chasing him, and nobody missing, and nobody to save. He felt as though he could finally sleep.

The hand came out of nowhere. Dan almost scissored out a powerful kick but was glad he didn't. Did breaking a conductor's kneecap get you thrown off a train in Italy?

The guy said something in Italian. Then the English penetrated Dan's foggy brain. "Ticket and passport. We're crossing the border."

"Oh. Sorry." Dan handed the conductor his ticket.

"Grazie."

"De nada," Dan said.

"That's Spanish," Amy whispered.

"No, it's *whatever*," Dan said. "I'm too tired to think."

"You guys slept through Milan," Vanessa said.

"Jet lag," Amy said. Her phone buzzed. By now Dan recognized the sound. It was the special phone Vesper One had sent to them, the phone that he used for his text messages. The DeOssie secure smartphone that was used by spies and soldiers. Vesper One had reconfigured it so that they couldn't reply to his messages.

He could always get to them. They could never get to him. The guy didn't play by the rule book.

Vanessa stood up. "I'm going to find some snacks. Anybody want anything?"

"Anything crunchy," Dan said. He handed her a couple of euros. "But if you can find American potato chips, we'll be friends forever."

She flashed a grin. "I'll work my mojo."

As soon as Vanessa started down the aisle, Amy scrambled for the phone in her pocket.

```
Lucerne is such a great place to shop.
While you're there, can you pick up a de
Virga mappa mundi for me? Don't worry,
you don't have to gift wrap it. I need it
soon, though. Four days from now, bright
and early. Or else.
```

"I wish this guy would stop making jokes," Dan said through gritted teeth. "And giving ultimatums. Do you know what *de Virga mappa mundi* means? Sounds like a pasta dish."

"*Mappa mundi* means 'world map,'" Amy said. She tapped out a quick text to their research team at the comm. center back home in Attleboro, Massachusetts. In a large attic room they had banks of computers, an array of handhelds, and sleeping quarters. They even had their own satellite, the *Gideon*. Amy had spent a fortune on a communications bunker in case something like this happened. She wasn't paranoid or psychic. Just wicked smart.

RECEIVED NEXT TARGET: DE VIRGA WORLD MAP.

In less than a minute, a reply came from her boyfriend, Evan.

GOT IT. ALL OK?

OK FOR NOW Amy tapped back.

Then she plugged the words *de Virga map* into the search engine on her smartphone.

"'The de Virga map is a medieval map of the world that was created in Venice between 1411 and 1415,'" she read to Dan. "It was discovered in Croatia in 1911." Amy frowned as she scrolled through the information. "Then it went missing for good, right before it was going to be put up for auction in Lucerne in 1932. It was withdrawn from the auction and nobody ever saw it again. Well, that explains why Vesper One directed us to Lucerne. We should head right for that auction house and see if we can get access to their records."

Dan frowned. "But how can we find a map that disappeared almost eighty years ago? That's impossible!"

"Haven't you gotten it yet?" Amy asked. "We're expected to do the impossible."

Dan looked at her bleakly. "And we're expected to do it fast."

The train slowed, then stopped. Dan pressed his face to the window. "What's going on?"

"It's okay," Amy said. "When we cross the border, sometimes they change personnel."

Dan watched as a group of train conductors left the small building and headed for the train. He relaxed back into his seat.

Then he shot forward again. Trailing behind the men and woman was a man in a shabby raincoat. A man with messy hair and sharp eyes . . .

"It's him," Dan told Amy. "He caught up to us. He's going to board the train!"

"I bet he's Interpol," Amy said, biting her lip. "We passed so far, but I don't know if we'll get by the international police force."

"Where is Vanessa?" Dan wondered. "She's our cover. I never thought I'd say this, but snacks just aren't that important!"

Just then the door at the end of the car opened. The man in the raincoat entered. He followed closely behind a train official, who politely asked a couple for their passports. Dan twisted and saw Vanessa heading down the aisle, her hands full of bags of chips and pretzels. She squeezed past the man and the train official.

Vanessa waved the bags at them cheerfully.

"Whew," Dan said. "She's back. Are you ready to be a Wowzabelle? I'll take the tuba, and maybe you can pretend to be asleep . . . we might fool him. How's your South Carolina accent, y'all?"

Amy gripped Dan's wrist. "That's it!" she exclaimed. "Something has been bothering me about that girl. When we first met her, do you remember how she introduced herself?"

"Sure. 'Hi, I'm Vanessa Mallory.'"

"'Vanessa Mallory from Wilmington, South Carolina.' Wilmington is in *North* Carolina."

Dan slowly turned to look at Vanessa. She was now blocked by a couple with a baby. Impatient to get by, she tried to help them with their stroller. Dan noted the tight, angry look on her face as she snarled a remark at the parents. Suddenly, her pretty face looked hard.

Suspicions started to flip through his brain like someone shuffling a deck of cards. Why had she been so friendly? How come she'd agreed to travel with them so quickly? It had seemed like they'd been the ones to approach her and offer to travel together, but did she set herself up to be approached?

They'd been played. By a *tuba*!

Amy grabbed her backpack. "Come on. We've got to get off this train."

CHAPTER 3

Location Unknown

"It hurts," Nellie said.

"I know," Reagan said. "No pain, no gain."

"Do you think they made that expression up for *bullet wounds?*"

If Nellie expected Reagan Holt, Olympic-level triathlete, to lighten up on her, she was dreaming. Nellie and Reagan were two hostages standing in a bare concrete bunker, but they might have been in an expensive health club for all the focus Reagan was bringing to the session. She'd refused to acknowledge that Nellie's bullet wound was any big deal ("Oh, please, it was more like a graze."), refused to concede that without proper equipment they couldn't train ("We've got a wall and a floor, don't we?"), and dismissed the idea that Nellie could be too weak to try ("There is no *try.* Only *do.* Yoda said that, and he was awesome.").

"Pain is pain," Reagan said. "Gain is gain. If you

don't rotate that shoulder, it will freeze up, and you'll be no help to anybody."

Nellie wanted to rotate it into Reagan's chin for a nice, satisfying sucker punch, but she knew her tormentor was right. She rolled her shoulder, letting out a hiss of pain.

Fiske Cahill winced and looked over at her sympathetically. In his jumpsuit he looked so pale and thin. She was used to seeing him in black jeans and sweaters, an elegant bohemian. Natalie Kabra stared vacantly at the same spot on the wall she'd been looking at for the past twenty minutes. Nellie was still waiting for Natalie's natural gifts as a schemer and a fighter to kick in. So far, no such luck. Alistair Oh lay back on the sofa, his eyes closed. In some ways, Nellie thought, the isolation and deprivation were hardest on Alistair.

No . . . they were hardest on Phoenix Wizard. Phoenix sat on the floor cross-legged, only a few feet away. He stayed close to Nellie now. He was only twelve years old and he missed his mother. He wouldn't say it out loud, but Nellie could see every bit of the sorrow and fear he was experiencing in his liquid brown eyes. She winked at him, then made a face behind Reagan's back. He grinned.

"You're doing great, Gomez!" Ted Starling cheered her on. He couldn't see her, but he could hear her grunts and hisses, Nellie knew. Ted had developed phenomenal hearing since he'd lost his sight. He always sat in a chair near the door, just in case he could pick up noises from outside. It was Ted who had determined that they must be underground.

"That's it. Gently now," Reagan said to Nellie. "We'll move on to the hard stuff tomorrow."

"This . . . isn't . . . the hard stuff?" Nellie spit out through gritted teeth.

Reagan grinned. "You really hate me right now, don't you?"

"Immeasurably."

"Good. Give me ten."

Nellie sighed. Her shoulder felt stiff. It ached. Her stomach felt empty. Whoever was preparing meals for the hostages had a rudimentary grasp of cooking. Peel potatoes. Boil. Serve. Nellie'd been enrolled in a cooking course in Paris when she got seized. She'd been about to enjoy a crisp, buttery croissant and a café au lait at her neighborhood café . . .

Do. Not. Think. About. Food.

Nellie pushed against the wall. She straightened her arms, then went forward again in a modified push-up.

"Excellent," Reagan said.

"Ow," Nellie grunted.

"Only nine more and you're done."

Reagan had dropped to the floor and was doing push-ups.

"Five . . . nine . . . ten!" Nellie said. She sank down against the wall, resting her head against it.

"I think," Reagan said as she moved up and down like a piston, "we should *all* have a plan to keep in shape." She jumped up and clapped her hands. "Okay, listen up, people. It's time we set up an organized schedule for exercise."

Alistair opened his eyes. "My dear, I haven't exerted myself in years."

"Then it's way past time to start, old man."

"I think it's a good idea," Ted said. "We need to keep our muscles active. And our minds. They're trying to play with our heads. Classic stuff. Strip us of our identities, not let us know what time it is . . ."

"Feed us carbs," Natalie said.

Nellie rolled her shoulder again. She felt perspiration break out at her hairline. She hated to admit it, but Reagan was right. They had to be prepared. There were things they could do.

"I'm going to work on individualized training plans for each of you," Reagan said. "This is going to be *awesome*!"

Alistair closed his eyes. "I was right," he said. "This *is* hell."

CHAPTER 4

Amy and Dan moved quickly through the train, adapting their gait to the gentle swaying motion. They passed through the doors into the next car and then the next. Amy glanced behind nervously. The conductor was moving swiftly. Behind him she saw the inspector. Had he seen them? Was he following them?

"We've got to find a place to hide!" she hissed to Dan. "He's gaining on us!"

Dan pointed to a door marked BAGAGLIO. "Remember that the guy said there was a place for oversized luggage?"

"But it's got to be locked."

Dan was already fishing in his backpack. He took a long, slender piece of metal and slipped it between the lock and doorjamb. He leaned in and wiggled it.

"What are you doing?" Amy hissed. "And whatever it is, hurry!" She glanced over her shoulder. The inspector was only a car away.

The door popped open and they quickly slipped inside. The small space was crammed with items:

bulging overlarge suitcases, trunks, boxes, and a pet carrier with an orange cat that hissed at them angrily.

Amy leaned against the door and waited for her heartbeat to slow. "Since when can you pick a lock?"

"Remember when you paid that security expert to give a seminar at our summer gathering?" Dan asked.

For the past two summers, Amy had gathered together the Madrigals, the under-the-radar branch of the Cahill family, at their mansion in Attleboro. After the race for the 39 Clues, the cousins who had been with Amy and Dan at the end—who had stood together to stop the Clues from falling into the wrong hands—all became Madrigals.

Amy had taken it upon herself to train them. She had also invited experts in all kinds of fields—rock climbers, computer software engineers, race car drivers, cryptologists—to give short seminars. She'd presented it in the spirit of fun, but she had a deeper purpose. For the past two years, she'd been preparing them for this. She and Dan had tangled with the Vespers before, and she'd known in her bones they'd be back. She'd dreaded it.

Only a few months after they'd returned from the Clue hunt, Fiske and Nellie had told them about a ring that the Madrigals had protected over the centuries. They'd gone to Switzerland with Fiske to pick up the ring from Grace's Swiss bank. There, the Vespers had stalked them. One of them, Casper Wyoming, had almost killed them. She never wanted to look into his cold eyes again.

She touched the black-faced Swiss watch on her wrist. The watch face now contained the ring. Hidden in plain sight. At least she could keep that safe.

"I remember," she said. "Lawrence Malley. He was an expert in security systems."

"Aka Lightfinger Larry." Dan grinned. "He was also wanted in five states."

"Great," Amy groaned. "I sent you to a tutorial with a crook."

"It got us in here, didn't it?"

"I guess I'm grateful to him, then," Amy said doubtfully.

"Don't be," Dan said. "The first lock I opened was on your diary. Don't worry, I read two pages and fell asleep."

Suddenly, they heard voices outside. Amy and Dan froze. A voice spoke in rapid Italian. The doorknob rattled. Amy looked around frantically, but there was no time to hide.

More Italian. Amy heard the word *chiave* — key.

A *smack* against the door, as if someone had slapped it in frustration. Then footsteps heading away rapidly.

"We'd better get out of here!" Amy whispered.

"Sure, but they can do the heavy lifting." Dan pointed to the large leather trunk of the fashionable Italian lady they'd seen at the station. "Are you thinking what I'm thinking?"

"I hope not," Amy said. "Because that would be a huge problem for me."

Dan was already using his metal device on the lock. It sprang open, and he lifted the lid. He began to toss out piles of ski clothes, shoes, dresses, and sweaters.

"What are you doing?" Amy asked. "This place looks like the mall during prom week."

Dan dug into his pack and came up with a multi-tool gadget. It had a hammer/pliers device on the top and a variety of knives and cutters concealed in the handle. "I bought this baby while you were looking for a charger for the DeOssie phone," he said. He began to use a tool to drill discreet holes in the trunk. "Nice trunk, but it'll be better with breathing holes."

"Both of us are going to fit in there?" Amy asked. "I don't think so."

"No, you're going in that," Dan said. He indicated a long nylon bag. Amy unzipped it and saw a snowboard.

"In here?"

"It's just until we get on a luggage cart. Then we'll get out. It's the only way. Look." He shook the luggage tag with the printed destination at her. "'Engelberg.' These are both getting unloaded at the next stop." Amy swallowed. Suddenly, the long black bag looked like a coffin.

Just then they felt it: the smooth deceleration of the train. There was no time to think of something else. Quickly, they stuffed the clothes behind a pile of suitcases. Dan climbed into the trunk.

Amy stuffed her pack and Dan's in the bottom of the bag, then quickly slipped into it.

She felt the snowboard digging into her back.

"But what if—"

He shook his head. "We don't have time for *what if*s. We haven't for a long time."

She looked into his intent green eyes. He was right. They had burst through all their *what if*s long ago, starting with the worst one of all.

What if Grace dies?

What if we can't find the clues?

What if we get caught?

What if we get killed?

Either things happened or they didn't. All you could do was deal with it.

Dan closed the trunk lid and Amy wiggled one hand out and latched it, then zipped herself into the bag. She closed her eyes and breathed. The air felt stuffy and she placed her mouth as close to the hole as she could. She felt the train come to a smooth stop. Footsteps approached in the corridor outside. She heard the door open.

She heard someone enter the car and circle it. Even the footsteps sounded careful . . . like the person would miss nothing. . . .

"*Niente,*" someone else said impatiently.

Niente . . . nothing. She was relieved to hear the train conductor argue something about the schedule. She could pick out random words in Italian, that was all.

She felt herself being lifted and tossed onto the luggage cart. The impact shuddered through every bone. Suddenly, she realized that other suitcases might be tossed on top of her. Maybe even the trunk! She panicked and reached for the zipper just as the cart began to move.

Her heartbeat tripped double-time. She was rolling now, and a bump told her she was off the train. She felt the rumble of the wheels. Then the cart stopped.

She eased down the zipper and tried to peer out. All she saw was hard blue sky. She felt the chill of mountain air. She eased the zipper down a bit more.

The train attendant was stepping back onto the train. A porter exited the Engelberg station, hurrying to meet the fashionable older woman surrounded by her suitcases. A young guy in a bright nylon jacket jumped off the train behind her—the snowboarder, Amy guessed.

The inspector stood on the step of the train, coolly surveying the station. Waiting to see if they'd disembark, she guessed. Any moment the porter would head this way to collect the bags.

Amy dared to unzip the bag a bit more. She could feel the sharp gaze and the stillness of the man just standing, looking . . . waiting.

Some late-arriving passengers hurried to board the train. The fashionable lady pulled out her cell phone and then pointed to the luggage cart, signaling to the porter that the large trunk was hers.

The train whistle blew. *Go. Go. Go . . .*

The train began to pull out, its speed way too slow for Amy.

She lifted her head slightly so that her eye was just above the zipper. The inspector still gazed out at the platform. At last he turned away and slipped back inside the train. With trembling fingers she unzipped the rest of the bag and wriggled out, then grabbed the packs and quickly zipped it back up. She was shielded from the porter by the stack of suitcases. She eased over to where the leather trunk lay and flipped the latches.

The trunk didn't open.

The lock in the middle had been clicked. The porter must have done it on the train.

"Dan!" she whispered frantically. "Can you hear me?"

"Open it!" She heard a thump as he kicked the top.

"I can't! It's locked!"

"Stick it!"

"Stick it?"

"Not stick it! Pick it!"

Amy glanced over quickly. The lady in the hat gestured for the porter to hurry. The young man had stopped at a vendor and was paying for a sausage roll. She had seconds before the porter would come for the trunk.

She dove for Dan's backpack. The slender piece of metal lay right on top of his rolled-up T-shirts. She stuck it in the lock and wiggled it. Nothing happened.

"It's not working!"

"Wiggle it!"

"I'm wiggling!"

Desperately, she reached for Dan's multi-tool. She shoved the metal pick between the lock and the trunk. She held it steady, then brought down the hammer with all her strength.

The lock blew. Springs rolled along the platform. The lock pinged as it hit the concrete.

Dan peeked out. "That's one way to do it."

"Come on!" Amy yanked on his arm, pulling him out, and slammed the lid shut. In another ten seconds, the porter would be there. "As soon as he sees the broken lock, he'll start asking questions. They could arrest us for stealing those clothes!"

Dan looked around quickly. "We've got to cross the tracks to the other platform."

They heard the sound of a whistle as a train began to roll into the station.

Amy paled.

"And we have to do it *right now*!" Dan grabbed his pack and shoved Amy's at her. She felt the vibration of the oncoming train under her feet.

A train began to slide into the station. They jumped onto the track. Amy felt as though she were moving in slow motion. All those months and months of hard training didn't seem to help her legs move when fear was draining her of strength. The people on the opposite platform turned slowly to look, their mouths open.

Dan pulled at her hand hard and she leaped the last few inches onto the next platform as the train roared into the station. The blast of air against her neck made her shudder.

She bent over double, catching her breath. The waiting passengers stared at them, shaking their heads.

"*Guten tag,*" Dan said cheerfully, and waved.

"We'd better get out of here before we attract any more attention," Amy murmured.

They quickly left the station and walked toward the center of town. "Let's contact Sinead and Ian," Amy suggested. "We can circle back to the station and catch a commuter train to Lucerne in a bit."

"Don't forget Evan." Dan batted his eyelashes at her. "*Oh, Evan, I missed you so. . . .*"

Amy ignored him, but inside she felt the instant flood of warmth that was caused by just hearing Evan's name. On the train, she had resisted the impulse to type *I miss you.*

Mostly, she missed talking to him and texting him without other people hearing and reading what she said. All of their text messages to each other were now public property. Evan was no longer just her boyfriend. He was practically an honorary Madrigal. He'd been enfolded into the group because of his tech knowledge, and he'd been invaluable so far.

They found a wooden bench under a stand of pines and sank onto it gratefully. For the first time, Amy realized that they were in an astonishingly beautiful place. The mountains rose above them, already white with snow. The town was picture perfect, with timbered buildings and roads free of cars.

"Why does Switzerland look like one big cuckoo clock to me?" Dan asked.

"Because you have no soul," Amy answered. "One of these days I'm going to come to a place like this and actually enjoy myself." She tugged at the blond wig on her head and stuffed it in her pack. "Wow, I'm glad to get rid of this."

Dan took off his glasses with fake lenses. "So who do you think that Vanessa Mallory was?" he asked. He fished out an apple from his pack and bit into it. "A cop?"

"She could have been working with the guy in the raincoat. It's hard to say."

"Better contact Attleboro. They might have a clue for the clueless."

Amy put her phone on speaker with the volume low and added a video feed so that they could see each other.

Sinead's face appeared on the screen. "Ames! I'm so glad you called. We weren't sure what happened to you."

"Sorry. We fell asleep on the train. Then we ran into a little trouble."

Sinead frowned. "Where are you now? Are you all right?"

"We're fine. Some little ski town close to Lucerne. We're catching the next train."

Suddenly, Sinead was shoved out of the way, and Ian Kabra filled the screen. "That's enough chit chat. Listen, we have news. We've got a Vesper ID for you from Cahills in the field. Erasmus did a cross-check and confirmed it. Vesper Six is Cheyenne Wyoming."

"Cheyenne?" Amy asked, her heartbeat speeding up. "Any relation to Casper?"

"Cheyenne is his twin sister. But I have worse news. Casper is definitely still alive."

Amy glanced at Dan. He looked as pale as she felt. Just hearing Casper's name brought back the fear.

Dan swallowed. "Bummer. And the guy has a twin? That's just wrong."

"I'm sending a photo to Dan's phone."

Dan reached for his phone. "Bring me the face of evil," he intoned.

"Any more information you can give us on the de Virga map?" Amy asked.

Sinead entered the frame. "We're checking some Cahill contacts in Switzerland. We think you should definitely start at the auction house where it was last seen."

"That's where we're headed."

Dan held up his phone. "Meet Cheyenne Wyoming."

Amy stared at the picture of a striking blonde. "Never seen her before," she said.

Dan studied the photo, then gave a start of recognition. "Oh, yes, you have," he said, bending over his smartphone.

"Amy?" It was Sinead. "I'm going to turn off the speaker. Evan wants to talk to you privately."

Amy turned off the speaker and pressed the phone to her ear.

"I just wanted to have a moment alone," Evan said. "Every time I talk to you, it feels like the whole world is listening."

Hearing his murmur, Amy felt as though Evan had just enveloped her in one of his comforting hugs. "I know," she said softly. "I was thinking the same thing. I'm so sorry that you got dragged into my mess. You didn't sign up for this."

"I *did* sign up for this," Evan said. Across the many miles, she heard the firmness in his voice. "You're in trouble. Do you expect me to just walk away?"

"I wouldn't hold it against you if you did."

"I know you wouldn't. That's only one of the reasons I'm crazy about you. I've got a million more."

"Just a million?" she teased.

"Okay, a million plus one—your cat."

She giggled. "You're bonding with Saladin?"

"Somebody has to protect that cat from your cousin Ian. And I even feed him. The cat. Not Ian. He's on his own. Anyway, if that doesn't get me Perfect Boyfriend status, I don't know what will."

"Emptying the litter box?"

"Hey. I have my limits."

Amy laughed. She had the phone pressed to her ear so tightly it burned. She closed her eyes, picturing his face. . . .

Ian's crisp voice broke in. "All right, lovebirds, let's move on. No offense, but I believe Amy and Dan might need a short course in style and class."

"Is this the nonoffensive part?" Dan asked. "I can't wait until you really insult us."

"Let's deal with reality, shall we? You don't just walk into an auction house in your jeans and backpacks. You have to blend in. And that's going to be hard." Ian sniffed. "Considering that you're Americans."

"What are you talking about, dude?" Dan asked. "This is my best SpongeBob T-shirt."

"Exactly my point," Ian said. "An auction is a place of taste and refinement. If you barge in looking like . . . well, *you* . . ."

"I get your drift, Ian," Amy said, cutting him off. "Do you know the most exclusive shop in Lucerne?"

"Of course. Here's an idea," Ian said. "Video your trip to the store, and I can advise you. Or else you'll emerge looking like a mushroom, and Dan like he just rolled out of bed."

Amy sighed. Just when she started to almost like Ian again — after all, he'd flown across the ocean and had been working around the clock to help — his snob quotient went through the roof.

She felt a sharp elbow in her ribs. Dan thrust his phone in her face. He had imported the photograph into a sketch program on his phone. He'd colored the bright blond hair brown and the eyes dark. He'd added a beauty mark above Cheyenne Wyoming's lip.

Amy gasped. It was Vanessa Mallory!

She quickly told the others what Dan had figured out. "But why was she tailing us?" she wondered.

"Vesper One wants to keep tabs on us," Dan said. "What else?"

"Remember, it's in his best interest to keep you two out of jail," Evan pointed out. "Maybe he sent her to make sure you got over the border."

"It's still creepy," Amy said.

"Speaking of creepy, she probably knows where you are right now," Evan said. "I've been looking at the manuals for the Vesper phone. I'm guessing that there's a GPS embedded in it, too."

Amy shivered as she glanced at the few pedestrians

walking by. Was Cheyenne watching them right now? Was Casper?

"Can we dismantle it?" she asked.

"You don't want them to know that you know it's there. But you can learn how to turn it off and on. You've got to be careful—it's got to look like satellite disturbance."

"Let Dan do it," Amy said. "He's better at these things than I am."

She handed Dan the Vesper phone. Dan tossed his apple core into the bushes. He pried off the back of the Vesper phone and listened to Evan.

"Yeah, yeah, I got it. Then what do I . . . oh, gotcha. Cool. Awesome! Take that, V-One!"

"Can we turn it off for a bit?" Amy asked.

"I think you can get away with it," Sinead said. "Just get to Lucerne as soon as you can. There's an auction at three. That can give you cover."

"Got it." Amy snapped the phone shut. She almost wished she didn't know about the GPS.

That meant that Vesper One could get to them anywhere. Anytime.

CHAPTER 5

Lucerne, Switzerland

Milos Vanek was tired. He was always tired. He relied on coffee to keep awake. Coffee and duty. He sat in the café on an upscale street in Lucerne. He'd chosen it for its large windows. He watched the crowd. You never knew when you could get lucky.

Tracing criminals . . . sometimes it was like a seed stuck in a tooth. Something that nagged him, some small detail that wouldn't go away. A crime would occur, a suspect identified, a search begun. Some were routine. And some were a seed in a tooth.

This brother and sister—Amy and Dan Cahill. He couldn't figure them out, and that was bothering him. Rich brats out for kicks? Most likely. Yet he dug a little bit and discovered that although they were fantastically wealthy they attended a public school, had not exhibited discipline problems, were not featured in the tabloids, did not give interviews, did not appear in a reality TV program . . . none of the things he expected.

Yet suddenly they had dropped out of school and headed for Europe. There was a small item in a Boston paper about a fuel truck and a school bus and a possible attempted kidnapping. It was the lack of detail that bothered him. Small article, then nothing. Schoolchildren had been endangered. Usually, Americans went crazy over things like that.

And within a few days these two kids had stolen a priceless painting from the Uffizi. A theft so cool and daring it must have been done by professionals.

But it had been done by children.

Then there was the strange accusation from an American student that Dan and Amy Cahill had stolen the first edition of Marco Polo's manuscript . . . a manuscript that didn't even *exist*. The accusation had been buried in a file, but Vanek had found it, because he didn't sleep much and he had a seed in his tooth.

They'd been on the Zurich train, he was sure of it. That's why he had the train stopped at the border. Somewhere between there and Lucerne, they had gotten off. But where did they get off? And *how* did they get off?

Kids could disappear more easily than adults. People didn't notice kids. And these kids were so . . . *neutral*. So bland in that American way.

His partner came out of the ladies' room. Most women when they exited a bathroom appeared with newly brushed hair, a fresh swipe of lipstick. Not Luna Amato. She went in looking like a slightly rumpled Italian grandmother and came out looking like a slightly rumpled Italian grandmother. Gray hair curling around her face. Black dress, flat shoes, unfashionable jacket with a coffee stain on the sleeve. Sharp brown eyes that could look vacant, kind, or merciless, depending on the situation.

He'd never worked with her before, but he needed someone who could blend in. Someone who could approach the kids and not scare them. He knew they'd been close to their grandmother, Grace Cahill. He'd been betting that they'd be suckers for someone her age.

Amato sat down and fished an ice cube out of her water glass. She plopped it in her coffee. He'd worked with her for three days now and the only thing he knew about her was that coffee was always too hot for her taste.

She took a sip. "Zurich," she said. "I think they went on to Zurich. They could have taken any number of trains from the station. The city is bigger. More places to fence the artwork. I say we head there."

Vanek nodded. She could be right. It was logical, a good deduction. And yet . . .

The seed in his tooth. The nagging feeling that they were close.

"You could be right," he said. "But first, let's see what we can find in Lucerne."

CHAPTER 6

"I can't do this," Dan said.

Amy and Dan stood on an exclusive shopping street in Lucerne. Steps ahead they saw the stone front of the expensive boutique Ian had told them about. One item hung on a skeletal hanger in the window, something black and tiny that appeared to be a dress or a tunic, or maybe a shirt?

If she couldn't even identify the clothing, how could she pass herself off as a fashionista?

"We just stole a painting and smuggled ourselves off a train," Amy said, trying to sound confident. "And we can't *shop*?"

"Don't make me." Dan gave her a mute look of appeal. "Can't you do it?"

"No." Amy felt her phone vibrate. She held it up. It was from Ian.

DON'T ASK THE PRICE OF ANYTHING. DON'T SMILE. DON'T SAY "DO YOU HAVE ANYTHING CHEAPER?" DON'T

Amy shoved the phone back in her pocket. "Just pretend to be Ian," she told Dan. "Come on, the auction is in an hour."

They pushed open the frosted glass door. There appeared to be about ten garments in the whole store, each separated by a foot of polished stainless steel rod. Amy stopped, confused. She was used to the cheerful jumble of fabrics and colors at the stores at the mall. But mostly she shopped on the Internet, finding one sweater she liked and ordering it in a couple of colors—usually navy, black, or gray. Last Christmas, when the Kabras had visited, Natalie's eyes had flicked over her sweater and skirt and said, "Is this a holiday, Amy, or did somebody die?"

When they had been enemies, Natalie would have punctuated the remark with a cruel smirk, but this time, she'd just shaken her head and laughed. And given Amy a beautiful wool scarf in a heathery blue for the holiday that Amy had worn every day.

Of course, a month later Amy had received the bill.

Dan was doing his best Ian Kabra impersonation, looking around the store as though inspecting it for cockroaches. Amy tried to turn her snort of laughter into a cough.

"Espresso?" The saleswoman materialized seemingly out of nowhere. Amy realized that the full-length mirror on the wall was actually a door.

If she were Amy Cahill, she would blush and shake

her head no, just because she didn't want to cause any bother. She imagined what Natalie Kabra would do.

"Tea. Darjeeling," she said in a curt tone.

"Oh, not Darjeeling, sis," Dan said. "That's just *so* middle class."

"Lapsang souchong?" the saleswoman asked.

"I just adored his last collection," Dan said.

The woman's tight smile dimmed. "That's a *tea*," she said through pursed lips. For the first time, her icy gaze traveled over their bulging backpacks and settled on their hiking shoes.

"Of course it is," Amy said. "My brother and I are on holiday," she added carelessly. "We came straight from boarding school and we're heading to our chalet, but Mummy has arranged some parties, and we thought we'd pick up a few things."

The woman appraised them coolly. It was clear that she didn't believe Amy at all. "Perhaps you'll be more comfortable in a department store."

Amy didn't reply. She remembered that about Ian and Natalie — they never reacted to something they didn't want to acknowledge. They just pretended the person hadn't said it at all. She handed the saleswoman a credit card. "Why don't you take this? We don't want to waste time. Just set up an account."

The saleswoman bit her lip. "I'll only be a moment," she said curtly. When she returned, she must have checked out the credit limit of the card, because she was wearing a wide smile.

"Please follow me," she said graciously. "My name is Greta."

Greta led them into a private room with plush sofas and a wall of mirrors. An empty rack lined the other wall. She disappeared again, then reappeared with an armload of clothes. Amy gulped. So this was how rich people shopped. They didn't even have to lift a hanger. They just had things brought to them.

For the next half hour, Amy and Dan almost drowned in silks, featherweight cashmeres, and supple leather shoes. Amy was overwhelmed, but she knew she needed to be efficient. Within thirty minutes they walked out of the store in new, impeccably tailored cashmere jackets, Dan in black and Amy in camel. Underneath she wore a green dress with heeled boots. Dan balked at the ties but chose a black sweater that Amy deemed Ian-worthy. The last thing Amy asked of Greta, now their best friend, was to call up a private car and driver.

"Do you know how much this purse cost?" she whispered to Dan as they sat in the backseat on the way to the auction house. She pointed to the large leather satchel on the floor. "More than a year at a fancy private school!"

"*Everyone needs a statement bag,*" Dan said, mimicking the saleswoman's accent.

Amy directed the driver to pull the limo up in front of the auction house. It was a white building that looked like a large manor house.

"It's too bad we couldn't get any images of the interior," Dan said.

The people going inside the heavy brass doors looked so . . . important. So self-assured.

I don't belong here, Amy thought.

A voice rose in her head. Nellie's voice. *C'mon, kiddo. You can do it. You're rocking the fancy threads. Work it.*

Amy smiled, but she felt her heart constrict. She missed Nellie so much.

The clothes helped. Even the ridiculously large purse the saleswoman had insisted she needed. She saw similar purses on the arms of the chic women walking through the doors.

She tried not to wobble in her heels as they walked into the lobby of the auction house. It was a double-height room with ornate moldings and a gleaming floor. Ahead was a grand curving staircase and to their right was a pair of double doors. A petite woman in a black suit and many strands of large pearls welcomed them in German, but when they answered she switched to flawless English. "Welcome. I am Frau Gertler. The auction will begin in ten minutes." She handed them a catalog. If she wondered what two teenagers were doing at an auction for Old Masters prints and paintings she gave no sign.

Dan moved closer to the woman. "I wonder if I might have a second catalog," he said. "Papa will be joining us. By the way, those are fabulous pearls. Mummy has a set just like them, but hers are slightly larger."

Amy nudged him. He was taking this Ian Kabra impersonation way too far. They had to blend in, not call attention to themselves.

"Thank you," Frau Gertler said, and leaned over to grab another small stack of catalogs.

The double doors to the auction room opened, and they glimpsed a large room with rows of gilt chairs. An empty easel sat on an elevated platform. People were filing in and sitting down.

Amy's eyes moved around the lobby. She saw now that many doors were tucked away in alcoves and underneath the stairs. Too many. Then she noted one that was marked BÜROS. She knew that was German for *offices*. She nudged Dan and pointed to it with her chin.

A group of people walked in and were greeted by the chic woman in the black suit. While she was occupied, they pretended to stroll and admire the moldings. They backed up against the door marked BÜROS.

"There's a slot for a key card," Amy murmured. "So I don't think you can work your lock-picking magic."

"That's okay," Dan said. "I have a key."

"How did you get that?"

"'*Fabulous pearls. Mummy has a set just like them,'*" he mimicked himself as he looked up at the moldings. Dan's face was set in a look of concentration Amy recognized. "I knew . . ." She sneaked a look and saw that behind his back Dan was trying to slide the card through the slot. ". . . if she leaned over . . . for the rest of the catalogs that I could . . . slip it out. . . ."

Amy leaned back. "About a fraction to the left and up an inch," she muttered.

Dan found the slot and slid the card in. The door opened a crack. With one last glance at the activity in the lobby, they quickly slid inside.

The door clicked shut behind them softly. Amy let out a breath.

"When did you turn into such a criminal? I didn't even see you move!"

"There's a fine line between criminality and genius," Dan said. "That's what Lightfinger Larry used to say."

The hallway was carpeted in severe gray. Steel-framed art marched down one wall. The offices on their left all had glass walls. They could hear the murmur of voices from behind a door to the right. Amy put a finger to her lips. They tiptoed down the hallway, slipping past the empty offices. They were lucky that it was a Saturday. The glass walls gave them a sightline into offices that looked like living rooms, with sofas and easy chairs and paintings on the walls. Amy stopped short.

"I think that's a Rembrandt," she whispered, pointing at a small dark painting on the wall of the largest office. "Isn't it amazing?"

"Sorry. Only one art heist a week for me," Dan said.

They tiptoed past and kept on going. Finally at the end of the hallway, a door on the right was marked REKORD-BÜRO. Amy nodded, and, after listening for a minute, they cautiously pushed it open. The office was empty.

"Whew," Amy whispered after they closed the door behind them. "Lucky. I think this is where the records are kept."

Unlike the elegant offices they'd glimpsed, this room was small and cluttered. A small desk with a fax machine was shoved in between a table and the door. The rest of the room was filled with filing cabinets. The old files could be right here.

"I don't think they would have digitized their transactions from eighty years ago. But they should have dead files."

Amy peered at the labels on the filing cabinets. "Bingo. These are the records from the 1950s. There are no records for the 1940s . . . they closed the business during World War Two . . . so . . . here!" She stopped before the last filing cabinet. "The records from the 1930s." She opened the drawer and groaned. "This could take a while. They aren't filed by the name of the object. It's by date. We know it's 1932, but we don't know what month." She handed Dan a hanging file. "Let's get started. We have to get this done before the auction is over so we can leave with the crowd."

She opened the first file. Records were kept in a tiny, neat handwriting. Amy slumped against the cabinet. "These are in German. Of course they would be."

"It's all right," Dan said. "It will still say 'de Virga.'"

She and Dan bent over the files. They had to keep the light off, so they used their penlights, flipping through paper after paper. Their eyes almost crossed trying to decipher the thin, spidery handwriting or faint type-writer ink, all written in a language they didn't know. Occasionally, they would freeze if they heard footsteps outside. Amy's palms were damp with nerves. If they got caught, what would they say?

Finally, just when *wild goose chase* was starting to dance around in Amy's brain, Dan whispered, "Got it."

He passed over a paper. Amy saw the words *de Virga* and *mappa mundi*.

Amy's heartbeat speeded up. Here it was, the original notes on the auction of the antique map. "I can't read the rest," she murmured. "But look—there's a list of names: 'Prof. Otto Hummel . . . Jane Sperling . . . Marcel Maubert . . . Reginald Tawnley.' And there's a notation next to each name."

"Doesn't Ian speak German?" Dan asked. "Maybe we can get a good enough resolution on a photograph to send it to him."

"Worth a try. And if he can't translate it, he can find a Cahill who can." Amy spread the sheet out on the floor and took a photograph with her phone. She e-mailed it to Attleboro.

A loud noise sent them shooting to their feet. Amy looked around wildly, but Dan laughed softly. "It's just the fax machine," he said.

"Make it stop," Amy groaned. "Somebody might come in. We're overstaying our welcome."

Dan crept over to the fax machine. "I wonder if it's somebody bidding on an Old Masterful." He mimicked a snooty British accent. *"I say, old chap, a million for that drawing of the cow. Make that two million. . . ."*

Amy stared down at the phone, willing it to chime an answer. When she looked up at Dan, he was staring at the fax in his hand.

"I think you're right about overstaying our welcome," he said. He walked over and handed her the fax.

INTERPOL MOST WANTED
AMY CAHILL DAN CAHILL

ALERT TO ART DEALERS, MUSEUMS, AUCTION HOUSES

BE ON LOOKOUT FOR TWO SUSPECTS. CONFIRMED THEFT OF CARAVAGGIO MEDUSA FROM UFFIZI. CONSIDERED TO BE PLANNING ADDITIONAL HEISTS IN EUROPE. BELIEVED TO HAVE CROSSED THE ITALIAN/SWISS BORDER. IF SPOTTED, CONTACT INTERPOL NUMBER BELOW.

6.13.1

"It's from some guy named Milos Vanek," Dan said. "He's the detective assigned to our case, I guess."

"Photos and descriptions," Amy said, looking at the next sheet. "This is not good." She stared at the photos on the paper. They were their real passport photos, so they had been taken a few years before. On the fax they were smudged and indistinct. One piece of luck, anyway. "This can't be the only fax machine in this place. We'd better get out of here."

They jumped again when Amy's cell phone vibrated. Amy pressed SPEAKER and Ian's voice rang out.

"Simple to translate," he said. "Easier than homework. Back in 1932, somebody at the auction house made a list of potential buyers for the de Virga. Those four names that have the little crosses and notations next to them? They were the clients that had to be treated with kid gloves. Hummel was a professor but he had family money. Jane Sperling was a socialite from Chicago. Maubert was an art dealer — there's an address in Paris — and the last one — Tawnley — was an Englishman who had a private library."

Amy looked at the names again. "Can you do more research on the names?"

"But why?" Dan asked. "We know they didn't buy it. It disappeared before the auction."

"It's the only lead we have," Amy said. She folded up the paper and slipped it into her pocket. "The auction house knew that these four people really wanted the de Virga. Maybe one of them stole it."

"We'll get back to you," Ian said, and hung up.

Activity in the hallway outside had increased. They could hear footsteps and voices.

"Come on," Amy said uneasily. "We'd better get out of here before somebody reads that fax."

When they cautiously cracked open the door, the

gray-carpeted hallway was empty. They swiftly made their way down it. When they turned the corner, a door to the right was open, and they saw Frau Gertler standing with her back to them. A man in a dark suit with an earpiece approached and handed her the fax.

Frau Gertler read the fax, then snapped it back to the security man. "Search the auction room," she ordered. "Discreetly. There are two teenagers here that could possibly be them. Just keep a sharp eye out." She hesitated. "My key card is missing. Better search the back rooms as well."

If Frau Gertler moved an inch, she would catch them out of the corner of her eye. Slowly, they began to back up.

Amy jerked her head. Next to them was a keypad. Dan took out the key card and swiped it through. The door opened and they slid inside and closed it. They were in the luxurious office they'd glimpsed earlier, the one with the Rembrandt on the wall. They leaned against the door to catch their breath.

"We've got to ditch this place fast," Amy said.

Dan hurried over and checked the windows. "They're sealed. We could break one, but . . ."

"Alarms." Amy said. Her gaze roamed over the office, and she found herself staring at the brown and amber painting on the wall. The Rembrandt.

Alarms, she thought again. Usually, they were trying *not* to trip them.

But this time . . . maybe an alarm could help.

CHAPTER 7

Amy slipped the Rembrandt off the wall and turned it over. Just as she'd hoped, there was a small electronic device stuck to the back.

"It's a sensor," she said. "Remember when we came in? There was a security checkpoint there."

"And we're going to set off an alarm?" Dan asked. "Um, pretend I'm stupid, because I'm not getting this."

Amy opened her new handbag, the one that had caused her to feel dizzy when she first heard the price. The only thing in it was a bag containing the rest of her lunch. She opened it up and placed the sensor inside the sandwich. "Someone else is." Quickly, she outlined her plan.

"Lightfinger Larry is going to come in handy again," Dan said after he heard it.

They peeked out through the glass walls. The corridor was empty for now. Quickly, they ran to the door leading to the lobby. Dan opened the door a crack. "The auction is over," he whispered. "People are starting to leave."

"That's good. We'll get lost in the crowd."

"Not for long. There's at least four security goons at the door."

"We've just got to give them a bigger problem to handle."

Amy pressed her eye against the crack. People were still clustering outside the auction room. Frau Gertler stood by, greeting customers, a tight smile on her face. Amy noted how her gaze darted around the lobby.

She quickly scanned the lobby, focusing on the fashionably dressed women.

A sleek blond woman stood close to the doorway, checking her smartphone. She had a raincoat slung over one arm and a replica of Amy's purse on the other.

"That one," she told Dan. "Ready?"

They slipped through the door and came up behind the woman just as she switched her handbag to her other arm in order to put on her raincoat.

"Allow me," Dan said, stepping up to assist her.

"Thank you, young man," the woman said approvingly in a French accent. "And they say American young people have no manners!" She twisted as Dan helped her on with her coat. Dan twisted at the same time, and the woman was suddenly tangled in her coat.

"Sorry!" Dan smiled winningly, and turned again, now pinning the woman's arm around her back as if by accident.

"Let me go, young man!"

"Sorry . . . just a minute. If I can just . . . get this around like . . . that . . ."

Amy moved up behind Dan. She was there to catch the handbag as it slipped down and quickly replaced it with her own. Without breaking stride she melted into the crowd.

"There you go!" Dan said, finally getting the woman untangled. "Have a *great* day!"

He caught up with Amy, but they slowed their steps, keeping their heads down and concealing themselves from the guards. The woman moved ahead of them. As she passed the security check, a piercing alarm sounded.

Frau Gertler's head jerked toward the checkpoint. She began to push her way through the crowd. Amy and Dan wriggled closer.

"May I see your handbag, madam?" the security guard asked.

"Absolutely not! This is absurd!" the woman protested.

The security man held his hand out. "Madam." It wasn't a question.

"What's going on?" a silver-haired man asked in English. Someone else asked something in French. Amy didn't need a translator to realize that rich people don't like to be prevented from doing what they wanted to do.

Frau Gertler checked the security screen. "It's the

Rembrandt," she said in a low tone to the guard. "We have to search the bag."

"Somebody stole a REMBRANDT?" Dan yelled. "What kind of security do you have here, anyway?"

"My Leonardo!" someone cried.

"Go ahead and search her, but I have an appointment!" Amy shrilled above the crowd's murmur.

"I have a plane to catch!" someone shouted.

"My driver is waiting!" a stout man insisted.

"Let them all go and detain this woman," Frau Gertler muttered.

Amy and Dan joined the crowd thronging toward the doors. As they passed through, they saw the security man hold up a sandwich.

"What is it?" Frau Gertler demanded.

"Ham and cheese, Frau Gertler," the man said.

"Aha!" the woman trilled triumphantly. "You see? I'm innocent! I'm a vegetarian!"

When they hit the cool air, Amy tossed the purse into the bushes and jumped in the car after Dan.

"Just drive," she told the chauffeur, and crashed back against the seat.

CHAPTER 8

FROM: V-1
TO: V-6
Remind me of your mission again? Oh, yes.
Surveillance of targets Amy and Dan Cahill.
That was it. Now enlighten me as to the
reason for your utter failure to complete
mission. Care to check in? Or would you
like to check out permanentemente, cara?

Vesper One slammed the phone down. Took a breath, then another. It was a shame he couldn't do everything himself. He had to rely on the Wyomings for muscle and surveillance. They were a ruthless pair. But they needed . . . prodding.

Fear was such a great motivator. Look at Amy and Dan, scampering around like hamsters, just for him!

The de Virga map was the piece needed for the next step. The thought of it made his palms itch. He could feel it dropping into his hands. Amy and Dan could do it. Given the right incentive, they could do just about anything.

In an odd way, he believed in them. Certainly, he was rooting for them. They would collect the pieces and he would assemble them, and then . . .

Eyes closed, he envisioned it all. What he would gain. Nothing less than everything.

Cheyenne Wyoming shoved her phone back in her purse as she swung down the Trüllhofstrasse in Lucerne. Vesper One was making threats. In his usual style, of course, calling her *cara*, an endearment in Italian, even while he was threatening to kill her.

It had taken her *years* to work herself up to Vesper Six. After Casper had totally botched the job in Zermatt, when he'd almost died trying to get the ring . . . well, she'd vaulted right ahead of him. Casper had been furious.

And even *she* didn't like to get on the bad side of her twin. The bad side was . . . extremely unpleasant. She rubbed her wrist absentmindedly. The fracture had required a small metal plate to repair the bone. Casper hadn't liked discovering he was out and she was in.

Just then a yellow BMW pulled over to the curb. "Hey, want a ride, fräulein?"

She stopped and shook her head. "Are you crazy, Casper? What are you doing in that car? Surveillance is supposed to be *covert*. That means nobody is supposed to notice you."

Her brother smirked. "Spoken by the tuba player of the Wilmington Wowzabelles?"

"Wasn't I right? Didn't the tuba totally draw them in?" She slid inside the car and had barely closed the door before Casper gunned the motor and took off. "Your timing couldn't be worse. I lost the Cahills. The GPS is all wonky. Satellite problems — it keeps going in and out."

Savagely, Cheyenne ripped off her dark wig and took the pins out of her long blond hair. She shook it and it cascaded down past her shoulders. Then she tossed her glasses out the window and popped out the dark lenses. She tilted the mirror and drank in the sight of her own baby blue eyes. She was herself again. Immediately, she felt calmer.

"I'm getting kind of sick of dancing to V-One's tune," she brooded. "And having V-Two breathing down our necks all the time, waiting for us to make a mistake."

"Word. And now you've played right into it. We might get dropped from the Council of Six."

Who's we, *bro?* Cheyenne wanted to say. I'm *the one in the Council. You don't even have a number anymore.*

But she couldn't say it. She still needed her brother.

"Now it's going to take us even more time to climb up the ladder," Casper continued.

She looked out the window as the picturesque streets of Lucerne slipped by. Streets with fancy stores with things in them that cost a lot. Things she wanted and deserved.

A plan was forming in her mind. "It doesn't have to take more time," she said. "Not if we're proactive."

A small smile began on Casper's lips. "Oh, sister-friend. I know that tone. What are you thinking?"

"If you want something, you take it," Cheyenne said, repeating what the two siblings had told each other from the beginning of their lives in crime. Back when their parents robbed banks, pulled scams, dragged them all over the country. Cheyenne and Casper had added Internet scams to the family's crimes, and they'd pulled in more than they'd ever dreamed. Soon they were known in the criminal underworld. And to the FBI and the police departments of various states. So when the Vespers came calling, Casper and Cheyenne were only too glad to ditch their parents (now serving twenty-five years to life) and join up with V-1. Now they weren't just criminals—they were *master* criminals, linked into a global network.

And she wasn't going to give that up for anybody.

"He thinks the Cahills can find what he's looking for," she said, tilting the mirror again to check out her image. "But what if *we* find it first?"

CHAPTER 9

The driver checked out Dan and Amy in the rearview mirror. It was the second time he'd done it in less than a minute.

Dan's fingers drummed nervously on the leather upholstery. He took out his cell phone and wrote a text to Amy.

DRIVER CHECKING US OUT. WHY?

Amy responded in seconds.

NOTICED IT TOO. WE SHOULD BAIL.

Casually, Dan pretended to adjust his backpack. Meanwhile, he looked over his shoulder. A sedan slipped in and out of traffic behind them. It speeded up to avoid a tram.

A tail? Or just an aggressive driver?

They were driving along the Reuss River now. Lucerne looked like a mashup of Zurich and Geneva and Zermatt to Dan—picturesque and impossibly clean, the streets full of law-abiding citizens. Wide, curving streets, buildings painted in pale colors. Everything looked fresh and pretty. It made him nervous. What he needed was a narrow, dirty alley to hide in.

Amy began to cough. She bent over.

"Amy? Are you okay?"

"I think I'm going to be sick," she said.

"Driver!" Dan called. "Pull over!"

The driver pulled over. Amy tumbled out, followed by Dan. She bent over, but her eyes swept the roadway.

"The dark blue car . . ."

"I know."

Amy wheeled and ran, Dan close behind her. He heard honking horns, and he looked behind them. The dark blue car squealed to a stop at the curb.

"They're coming!" he told Amy.

They turned down a side street, then another. Dan could see that Amy was struggling. His sister could barely walk in high heels, let alone run.

The road curved, and suddenly they were at the river again. It was a crisp fall day, and people were strolling along the walkway. Dan and Amy weaved through the crowd, trying to put distance between themselves and whoever had been in the dark blue car.

"Dan," Amy called, "I twisted my ankle!"

She limped behind him. Dan saw something ahead, a crowd of tourists listening to a guide in front of a wooden covered bridge that spanned the river.

"Just a few feet more," he said. "Hurry."

They melted into the crowd.

"One of the most famous landmarks in Lucerne, the Chapel Bridge, or Kapellbrücke, is the oldest wooden bridge in Europe. . . ."

Dan nudged Amy. They skirted the tourists and began to walk across the bridge. *Clomp, clomp* . . . their footsteps echoed underneath the wooden roof.

"Are you okay?" he whispered to Amy.

"I can make it. I just need to sit down soon."

"Okay. When we cross the river, we'll stop."

Clomp, clomp . . . their footsteps mingled with the sound of the tourists entering the bridge behind them.

One pair of footsteps was walking faster than the others.

Dan stiffened. He pressed Amy's arm, and they moved a bit faster.

Clompclomp. Clompclomp.

And the footsteps behind them moved faster.

Clompclompclomp.

Faster yet. And the footsteps behind them echoed their hurry.

"Dan . . ." Amy was close to sobbing.

He pressed her forward.

Clompclompclompclomp.

The footsteps were running now. The person was immediately behind them.

Dan suddenly broke off from Amy, turned, and

barreled into the figure following them, straight into a stomach. He heard the surprised *oof* and he kept going, slamming the person into the wooden railing of the bridge, lifting him at the same time in a move that would get a halfback thrown out of the Super Bowl.

He just had enough time to see William McIntyre's surprised expression as their family lawyer flipped backward over the railing and into the Reuss River.

Mr. McIntyre sat in the back of the dark blue sedan, wrapped in blankets. His teeth were still chattering. Dan refilled Mr. McIntyre's mug with more hot chocolate from a thermos.

"I'm getting too old for this," he said.

"I'm really sorry," Dan said. "I just thought . . ."

"You could have called out," Amy said.

"I didn't want to use your names," Mr. McIntyre said. "And I couldn't remember which alias you were using. They know you're in Lucerne. I needed to get you out of the city as soon as possible."

"So where are we going?" Amy held out her cup and Dan poured her more hot chocolate.

"Basel. Third largest city in Switzerland. You can hide there for a bit. There's a place I know where you'll be safe. Get a good night's sleep. You look like you could use it." He looked at both of them. "This is different from the thirty-nine clues. You're not on your own. You have a solid team behind you. So reach out." He smiled. "Just don't reach out and push me into a freezing river next time."

"I'll try to remember that." Dan grinned.

Outside the windows, the soft rain made the air look like silver mesh. The wet streets gleamed. Amy snuggled under the soft wool throw. Mr. McIntyre always made her feel safe, with his kind gaze and gentle, deep voice. Only he would think to pack a thermos and blankets in case of trouble.

She was so glad he hadn't been kidnapped, too. If they lost all three of them — Fiske, Nellie, and Mr. McIntyre . . . it was unimaginable. Amy pushed the thought away. She was here, and warm, and cozy, and she breathed in the comfort Mr. McIntyre always brought her.

Amy sighed. "I don't know if I can sleep until I figure this out."

"Attleboro has already begun to research," McIntyre reassured them. "And I brought a treat." He reached down to the floor of the car and plopped a black nylon bag on the seat. He removed what looked like a large stainless-steel watch. He flipped up the face of it and they saw a digital map with a green dot on it. "This is a wrist GPS device. And it has an audio component if you need it — so that it can talk you through a route. Comes with an earpiece, too."

"Awesome," Dan declared, reaching for it.

"It's already configured to our *Gideon* satellite.

You can load your info onto it using this flash drive," McIntyre said. "After you load it, destroy the drive."

Amy felt the next few days open like a dark hole she was about to fall into. She shook off the feeling and concentrated on the object in Mr. McIntyre's palm.

"This is all so cool, Mr. McIntyre," Dan said. "I feel like a superspy."

McIntyre hesitated, and for a moment the tall, gray-haired man looked almost boyish. "After all this time . . . don't you think you could call me William?"

Amy and Dan exchanged glances. As fond as they were of him, they couldn't imagine calling their lawyer by his first name.

He saw the hesitation on their faces. "Will?"

Amy cleared her throat. Dan fiddled with the new GPS.

"How about 'Mac'?"

"Mac," Dan said, trying out the name.

Mr. McIntyre looked wistful. "I always wanted to be a Mac."

"It's perfect, Mr. McIntyre." Amy said. "I mean . . . Mac."

"I just have to say one more thing." Mr. McIntyre loaded the devices into Amy's backpack. Then he looked at each of them in turn.

"I am very proud of you two. Grace would be, too."

Amy's eyes misted. She leaned forward and hugged Mr. McIntyre. That didn't feel awkward at all.

CHAPTER 10

Attleboro, Massachusetts

Evan sat in front of the computer in the command center attic, his head resting in his hand. It was midnight. The house was quiet. Even Saladin was asleep on a stack of papers.

Sinead slipped through the doorway and came to sit in the chair next to him. "You should get some sleep."

"I want to be here when she wakes up."

"Don't your parents wonder where you are?"

"They think I'm in a sleepover study group. As long as I say the words *Harvard* and *extracurricular*, they're on board."

Sinead snorted. "Look, they didn't get to Basel until midnight. When she contacts us, I'll wake you up. There's a six-hour difference—it's only six A.M. there."

Evan shook his head. "I'll crash on the floor if I need to. She's going to want all this information as soon as she wakes up. And there's stuff I can do while I wait."

"There's always stuff we can do," Sinead said. "But

if we work ourselves to exhaustion, we can make mistakes. And that doesn't help anyone."

He knew she was right. Around him the blue screens of the computers glowed. The monitors from locations around the world were temporarily dark. Tacked to the walls were printouts from their research. Sinead had put up six bulletin boards, one for each Vesper in the Council of Six.

They had run out of space on the wall, so Evan had strung a wire from one end of the room to the other. They'd begun to clothespin random pieces of information from Cahill texts around the world.

Rumor of Vesper activity
10 years ago in Malta
Megalithic temples

Nellie Gomez landlord surveillance.
Landlord cleared of possible role
in kidnapping. Investigate other
students at cooking school?

One after the other, the pages fluttered like flags in the slight breeze from the heating ducts. Impossible to tell which should be investigated, and in what order.

Evan rubbed his forehead. "That note that Amy and Dan found from their grandmother. *VSP 79 – Pliny described first test.* How could all this circle back to some volcanic eruption back in Italy in A.D. 79?"

"We don't know. But we'll find out."

Her tone was confident. It reminded him of Amy's.

Evan had been plunged into the Cahill world like a deepwater pool, and he was still trying to stay afloat. He still couldn't quite get over the fact that his girlfriend, whom he thought of as shy and reserved, actually had the skills of an international spymaster.

And Sinead—he had met her plenty of times. She was Amy's best friend, but he had found her distant and chilly. He'd often felt that he kept failing to pass a test she hadn't explained to him. But now that they were working together, he realized that she just had a hard time letting people in. And no wonder—Amy had told him that Sinead's two brothers had been severely injured in a freak explosion in Philadelphia more than two years ago. Now he knew that the explosion was certainly Cahill-related, but he couldn't find the courage to ask Sinead about it. Her brother Ted was one of the hostages. No doubt that was what gave her such incredible drive.

Sinead came over and put her hands on his arms. She gave him a shove. "C'mon. Go sack out. I'm going to run a few programs. I promise to get you if Amy checks in."

He stumbled to his feet. He felt like his eyes were full of sand. "Okay. I'll catch a few hours."

Sinead's green eyes were steady on his. "I never knew how much you cared about her until now."

He nodded. "Me, neither. I'll do anything for her."

Sinead nodded. "Me, too," she said softly.

CHAPTER 11

Basel, Switzerland

Dan woke in a panic, forgetting where he was. He lay for a long moment taking in the room, the flowered duvet on the twin bed, the flowered wallpaper, the flower painting on the wall, the vase of roses. . . .

Gartenhaus. The small inn on a side street in downtown Basel. Mr. McIntyre—Mac—had left them here last night, urging them to get some sleep. He had to head off to see a client in Rome.

Dan glanced at his sister, curled up like a comma in the other bed. A perfect time to grab a shower before Amy monopolized the bathroom.

He stood under the spray. Despite its warmth, he still felt chilled. Every time he closed his eyes he saw Nellie's face, white with pain.

No more deaths, he thought. *If I have to live through one more death, I'll fall apart.*

He knew what he had to do. Change the odds.

When he emerged, he gave the smell test to a T-shirt

in his pack and pulled it on, along with his jeans.

He heard a groan from the other room and stuck his head out the door.

"I'm so hungry," Amy said sleepily.

"Hey, you stole my line," Dan said.

There was a soft knock at the door. They both tensed.

"Breakfast," the landlady called softly.

Amy opened the door and Frau Stein bustled in, carrying a tray laden with rolls, cheese, sausages, eggs, jam, a pot of coffee, and a pitcher of hot chocolate.

"I heard the stirring. I don't know what you like, so I brought everything," she said.

Dan took the tray. It smelled like paradise on a plate. "Thank you a bazillion times."

"I don't know this *bazillion*, but you are welcome." She smiled and walked out.

Amy and Dan attacked the food. In mere minutes, the plates were clean and they were sitting, stuffed, with cups of hot chocolate. The food and sleep had helped. They were raring to go. But where?

"We've only got three days left," Amy said.

"And counting."

Amy spread out the paper she'd taken from the auction house. She ran her fingers over the names. "A professor, a socialite, an art dealer, a guy with a private library. Just what you'd expect. And they all have money. So why would one of them steal it?"

"And why would it stay hidden?" Dan asked. "It's been eighty years. Why hasn't someone found it? Why hasn't someone tried to sell it? It doesn't make sense."

Amy frowned. "Attleboro has probably researched these names already." She reached for the computer. In a moment they saw Evan's concerned face. Sinead was right at his shoulder.

"McIntyre told us that he brought you to a safe house," Evan said. "I'm glad you got to crash. We have some background information. Are you ready?"

"Ready," Amy said.

"Let's see . . . Marcel Maubert and Reginald Tawnley both died during the war. But this is interesting—the German professor with all the dough? He became a big guy in the Nazi party. He killed himself—or maybe someone killed him—after the Allies took Berlin in 1945. And Jane Sperling—she was a socialite—her father was Max Sperling, who had a chain of department stores in the Midwest. She was also a medieval scholar—studied at the University of Chicago and then went to Germany. We're betting that she knew Hummel, because she studied in Heidelberg at the university there."

"Heidelberg," Amy said. "Wasn't that where the family who owned the de Virga was from?"

"That's right. Interesting coincidence, isn't it?"

"What happened to Jane Sperling?"

"She moved to London. During the war she worked for the War Department as a secretary. Later, after the war, she married a GI in Maine. Led a quiet life."

"So there's not much there," Dan said.

"We'll turn up something," Sinead said.

"We just have to keep digging."

"Have we heard anything from Vesper One?" Dan asked.

"Nothing," Evan said. "As far as we know everyone is still okay."

They were silent for a moment. Remembering faces. Remembering how far Vesper One was willing to go.

"Well," Amy said. "Let's get moving."

Dan hung up the phone. Amy bent over the paper, her finger moving back and forth over the names.

She looked up at him. "We're on the wrong track."

"I didn't know we *had* a track."

"We keep focusing on the map itself. We should be thinking about the world *around* the map. What was going on in Europe at the time? What did all those names have in common?"

"They were all rich," Dan said.

"The war," Amy said. "It was 1932. World War Two was still years away. But the world was gearing up for it. The Nazis were coming to power in Germany."

She accessed a search engine on the computer. Dan looked over her shoulder. "What are you looking for?"

"No idea," she murmured. "But sometimes you have to go fishing."

He saw her type in *Jane Sperling*, then start to scroll through material. "Interesting," she said. "Jane Sperling was Jewish. Did she know her teacher was a Nazi? Hang on." She tapped a few more words into the computer and then turned back to Dan. "Just what I thought. The Nazis took over the government in 1933. Jewish students were pressured to leave universities as early as 1932. Eventually, the Nazis expelled Jewish students from every university in Germany."

"I didn't know that part," Dan said. "Those guys were nasty dudes."

Amy looked up. "Why was she at the same auction as her Nazi professor? Coincidence? I just don't buy it."

He tried to follow Amy's logic. He'd learned about World War II and the Nazis in school, had read books about it. But to put himself in the heads of the people who actually lived the horror of it — that was harder. Amy had a gift for it.

"She was a young girl alone — she was only nineteen," Amy continued. "You can bet her parents wanted her to come home. Germany was turning into a scary place for Jews. But she stayed. She stayed, Dan!" Amy smacked the pillow next to her. "She had courage. So, maybe she knew that her Nazi professor was coming to bid on a famous historical document. The family who owned the de Virga was Jewish. Maybe she was trying to protect it!"

"So why didn't she just buy it? She was rich."

"Maybe she was planning to. That's why she came to Lucerne — to outbid Hummel and the others. But somebody got to it first," Amy said.

"Hummel?"

Amy's fingers flew as she typed an e-mail. "I'm asking the Attleboro group to research Hummel. Then we'll dig a little deeper into Jane Sperling. I just have a feeling these two are connected somehow."

Dan knew better than to argue with Amy's feelings.

"Look, research isn't my strong suit," he said. "How about I go out and gather some more supplies for us?"

Amy waved a hand. She was already gone, lost in the 1930s and the lives of people she'd never meet.

"Back in an hour," Dan said.

He had already done a quick search on the train, using his smartphone. He knew he didn't have much time. He'd managed to gather seven ingredients in Italy. If he could find a few here in Basel—three, at least—he'd have one-quarter of the serum ingredients. And some ingredients he could save for last, things he could pick up easily at any grocery store: salt, mint, honey . . . those would be easy.

He blended in like a tourist in his jeans and jacket and baseball cap. He stopped in a pharmacy and in five minutes flat had left with a small bottle of iodine.

Amy would be furious—and concerned—if she knew he was assembling the serum. She was afraid of it. She would never allow him to take it. She would say it would change him—possibly kill him.

What she didn't understand was that he didn't care.

The darkness was just . . . there. Sometimes it scared him. Sometimes it made him angry. An anger he didn't know he was capable of, something bottomless. Seeing

Nellie wounded and scared had seared him. Just days ago he'd held a dying girl in his arms, a stranger who had trusted Vesper One.

Amy didn't realize that you had to fight with everything you had. Not just your nerve and your courage, but the secret, hard, dark places inside you.

He plugged the next address into his GPS. He had found a place, a chemistry supply company willing to sell mercury and phosphorus. He hopped on a tram and took it to the outskirts of the city, an industrial area with warehouses and office buildings.

He found the address and rang the bell on the steel door. A moment later the door opened. A man, probably in his twenties, peered out and asked him something in German.

"Guten morgen," Dan growled.

"Oh, you're American. And a Yankees fan."

Dan touched the bill on his cap nervously. "I'm the one who contacted you about the . . ."

"Yes. Come in."

He was led into a small office. The man held up a glass vial. Dan saw the molten mercury.

"Toxic," the man said. "You know this? You must be careful how you handle it."

"I know," Dan said. "You wouldn't have liquid gold, would you?"

"Colloidal gold? Yes . . . how much would you need?"

"Quarter ounce should do it."

The transaction was completed in minutes. Dan

shifted as he counted out the bills. He could feel the man's eyes on him.

"So. You must be a New Yorker," the man said. "I love New York. *The Lion King*—excellent show!"

Dan turned to go.

"I don't think I caught your name," the man said.

"I didn't throw it," Dan said.

He left the place and walked quickly back to the tram stop. On the way, he tossed the Yankees cap into the trash can. Too many questions. The guy was probably harmless. But he couldn't take a chance.

Vesper Two read the text message and smiled.

Dan Cahill had made several interesting purchases while in Basel. Sending out that alert to all chemical supply houses had been a brilliant stroke. Amazing what the promise of a little money could do. If someone comes asking to buy odd items, please let us know. We will make it worth your while.

So, just as Vesper Two had thought. He was collecting the Clues, thirty-nine ingredients for the serum.

The serum could change everything. And the only one who had the formula was Dan Cahill.

Vesper One didn't have to know just yet. He wasn't convinced that Dan could be turned. Not yet. He didn't realize completely that the ties of blood could work in their favor.

Not yet. But soon.

CHAPTER 12

Amy leaned back and rubbed her eyes. She had window after window of research stacked on her computer. She'd spoken to Evan and Ian and Sinead. They'd thrown theories at each other, random facts, odd bits, wild guesses, hoping something would stick. Nothing did.

"Talk to me, Jane," she said aloud. "You were a rich girl, used to comfort. London was being bombed. Why did you stay? Why did you stay in Germany so long in the thirties? *Who are you?*"

She typed in *Jane Sperling* and *World War II* and scrolled through the results. She clicked on a page called Down Easterner, a small-town paper in Angel Harbor, Maine. Amy quickly scanned the article, an obituary for Jane Sperling. She had died at age ninety-two. The obituary documented her early life, her studies at the University of Chicago, and then the war years.

"*Yes, I stayed in London during the Blitz. Oh, heavens, I was never heroic. Just a secretary for the OSS—I translated documents and things from German to English. Because*

I'd lived in Germany before the war. I never look back. The things I did are done now. All down the drain."

"OSS," Amy muttered. She did a quick word search. The Office of Strategic Services was the spying arm of the American government during the war!

Amy clicked back to the research Evan and Ian had sent. Professor Hummel had turned out to be one superbad Nazi. He'd risen to major and had been involved in a group called the *Einsatzstab Reichsleiter Rosenberg*, which, as Evan put it, was quite a mouthful for "dirty despicable thieves." They were also known as the ERR, Hitler's special group that stole art and artifacts and property from Jewish families. The artworks were shipped to Paris and stored at a museum called the Jeu de Paume. There, the art was cataloged, inventoried, and crated, then sent to Germany. Hundreds of thousands of looted treasures from world-famous artists: Leonardo da Vinci, Michelangelo, Rembrandt, Van Gogh. Hummel was a high-ranking officer in charge, valuable because of his knowledge of medieval art.

"So, Herr Hummel," Amy murmured, "you were a thief."

Near the end of the war, as the Allies began bombing German cities, the Nazis got nervous. They moved the art to salt mines and caves and castles in the Bavarian Alps. It all would have worked except for a few inconvenient facts. One: The Nazis lost the war. Two: In 1943, a section of the Allied army was formed called the Monuments Men. After the invasion they traveled with the front lines, charged with finding the artworks and returning them to their rightful owners.

"The Nazis were evil, but what made them so especially chilling is that they were really *organized* about it," Evan had explained. "They kept records of everything they stole. So when the Allied armies moved in, they found everything—hidden caches of priceless paintings and artifacts. . . . If Hummel had the de Virga, there should have been a record of it. But there's nothing. It's another dead end."

"Maybe," Amy murmured now to herself. She typed *Monuments Men* and *Otto Hummel* into the search engine. If the US Army was chasing stolen art, they must have known about Hummel.

A document popped up on Hummel's death. His body had been found by a group of Monuments Men as the war was ending. He had been shot and was still sitting in a gilt chair in the ballroom of Neuschwanstein Castle, the famous site built by King Ludwig II of Bavaria, often called the Mad King.

The Monuments Men had been acting on information from one American spy, code name Sparrow, who had traced thousands of artworks looted from Jewish families all over Europe to Neuschwanstein Castle.

Amy read through a record of a soldier who had served there. *"We had a strong suspicion that Sparrow had killed Hummel,"* he said.

Amy rubbed her forehead. Everything was jumbled together in her head. Spies and stolen art,

Nazis, heroes, victims. A medieval map. How was it all connected? Was it connected at all?

She just *knew* the answer was here.

She contacted Attleboro again. Ian answered.

"Can you help me out with some research?" she asked. "I need to know the identity of a spy at the end of the war called Sparrow. He might lead us to Jane."

"You know," Ian said. "That's a funny coincidence. . . ."

"What?"

"Sparrow is *Sperling* in German," Ian said.

"Of course!" Amy sat up. "It's Jane! It's got to be! We need confirmation."

"I'm on it," Ian said.

Amy checked her watch. Where was Dan? He'd been gone for way over an hour. Just as she had the thought, he walked in.

She examined him briefly as he tossed his backpack on the floor. That mask was there. He had gone deep inside himself. Whenever she saw it, it chilled her. It was like she had lost her brother.

"I think we found the connection between Jane Sperling and Hummel," she told him. "I think she killed him!" Quickly, she explained that she thought Jane Sperling had been a spy for the OSS.

"Sparrow was chasing Hummel. I think she was still tracking the de Virga. What if the de Virga was at Neuschwanstein Castle? They were both there at the same time—that can't be a coincidence!" Amy insisted.

Ian broke in. "We just got a confirmation from a Cahill in the field—our government source. He's confirmed that Jane Sperling was Sparrow."

"Yes!" Amy exclaimed.

"Neuschwanstein Castle is a Janus stronghold," Sinead said. "We can definitely get you a schematic of the interior and send it to your wrist GPS."

"And we'll send Hamilton and Jonah in for backup," Ian said. "They're already in the air flying back to Europe. We'll have them fly into Munich."

"I don't know about this, Ames," Evan said. "You're building a case just based on guesses."

"Not guesses," Amy said. "Instinct."

"And I trust Amy's instincts," Dan said. "I say we go."

"Dan's right," Sinead said. "We trust you, Amy."

Apprehension suddenly bloomed in Amy. Despite their confidence—or maybe because of it—she was afraid.

Sometimes this felt so surreal, like she'd walked into an alternate universe. Maybe the real Amy was back in Attleboro, Massachusetts, a nerdy grind who got excited over research papers and whose idea of a big day was whipped cream on her chai.

That Amy didn't lay everything on the line and say *we have to do this.* And that Amy didn't have a gut-wrenching fear staring her in the face every moment—that she wouldn't be smart enough, or brave enough, to save the lives of the people she loved.

CHAPTER 13

Location Unknown

"Fifty-four, fifty-five, fifty-six . . ." Reagan rapped out. She wasn't even winded.

Nellie struggled with the next sit-up. Alistair had collapsed at seventeen. Fiske had kept up until forty. Natalie was humming to herself as she moved. Ted was concentrating, perspiration on his forehead. And Phoenix was following Reagan easily.

"Sixty. Good job, people. Done for the day."

"Thank you," Alistair breathed.

"All right," Reagan said. "Tomorrow we'll tackle shoulders and arms. That means push-ups, people! And if you want to fit in some extra ab work after dinner, I'll be cranking out some more crunches."

At the mention of dinner, Nellie's stomach growled. "Please don't mention food," she said.

Just then they heard the sound of the dumbwaiter shuddering down. Fiske went over and lifted the panel. "Cabbage and potatoes," he said.

Nellie shook her fist at the camera closest to her. "Hey, bozos!" she yelled. "Get a decent chef!"

"Yelling doesn't work, remember?" Fiske said mildly. He took out the casserole dish while Alistair set out paper plates. "The last time you complained about the food, we got bread and water."

"I know," Nellie said. "I'm sorry. It's just that . . . what I wouldn't give for a *poulet rôti aux herbes*. With crispy *frites*. And I'd really like to see the look on the French waiter's face when I ask for ketchup."

"I miss salad," Natalie said.

"Cookies," Phoenix said.

"Sushi," Fiske said.

"Bibimbap," Alistair put in. "Or a chicken burrito with chipotle sauce."

"Grilled cheese sandwiches," Ted murmured. "With pickles."

Everybody stared down at the cabbage and potatoes on their plates.

Fiske picked up his fork. He took a bite. "Delicious."

They all exchanged glances. There was nothing to do but eat.

Nellie chewed the overcooked potatoes and the limp cabbage. The casserole dish was scraped clean. Their kidnappers were not generous with portions.

The casserole dish . . .

Someone had made a mistake. Their first mistake.

The casserole dish was made of ceramic. Usually they sent food in plastic containers.

Nellie noted that Fiske's gaze had followed hers. She saw the same idea light up his eyes. Their gazes met.

Me, Nellie silently asked Fiske . . . *or you?*

Me. It had to look like an accident. With her shoulder injury, it just might work.

She dropped the plastic spoon onto her empty plate, then stood. She walked over to the garbage in the corner and tossed them into the container — no recycling for these kidnappers. Then she picked up the casserole dish and started toward the dumbwaiter to return it.

"Ow!" she suddenly cried, as though her shoulder had given her a terrible twinge. Her hand jerked, and she dropped the dish. She was sure to release it with force. It shattered, the pieces shooting across the floor. A huge shard skittered to a stop against Ted's foot.

"Sorry!" she called. She bent down and retrieved the pieces. Alistair got up to help, as well as Fiske, Phoenix, and Reagan. Only Natalie continued to eat.

Ted casually put his foot on top of the shard.

They dumped the broken pieces in the dumbwaiter, shut the panel, and returned to the table. One by one, they got up and threw away their plates. Phoenix cleared Ted's, the way he always did.

Ted's foot remained on the shard.

Things had changed. Now they had a weapon.

CHAPTER 14

Munich, Germany

"Dude," Hamilton Holt said.

"Dawg," Jonah Wizard said. They knocked knuckles. "We're on the case again, bro."

They had just touched down at Munich Airport in Jonah's private jet. Jonah had already rented a car; it would be fastest to drive to Neuschwanstein Castle, especially at the speed he could hit on the autobahn. It took only minutes for Jonah and Hamilton to pass through customs, load their luggage, and swing into the red sports car.

"We are officially on celebrity time," Jonah said, adjusting the side mirror. "No lines for the Wizard."

Hamilton awkwardly folded himself into the passenger seat. "Couldn't you get something bigger?" he asked as he banged his knee against the dashboard.

"We're supposed to be a diversion," Jonah said. "Got to make an entrance. Can't do that in a minivan,

Giganto Boy. Can't do much of anything in a minivan except look about as uncool as it gets."

"Hey! My dad drives a minivan."

"Snap."

"I guess I get your point," Hamilton said as Jonah floored the accelerator. Eisenhower Holt was not known for his hipness. He was known for smashing the family recyclables into neat little piles. With his head.

"I took a racing car driving course from a NASCAR dude for my movie," Jonah said. "I spent a week learning defensive and offensive driving." He squealed around a corner.

"That's great," Hamilton said. "But can you drive like you're not trying to kill me?"

They zoomed onto the autobahn. Jonah slipped a CD into the player and the sounds of "Your Love Makes Me So Fly (More Than Money)" came booming out. Hamilton had to restrain himself from reaching for the earplugs he'd worn on the plane. Jonah's music was loved by millions all over the world, but it was a mystery to him. It sounded like noise with a bass line.

He endured three CDs before they were zipping closer to the foothills of the Alps, through scenery that even Hamilton had to admit was stunning. He appreciated power shakes and great football tackles and the way you feel after a forty-mile bike ride. Scenery wasn't there to be admired, it was there as a backdrop for climbing, running, rowing, and picking up large objects and throwing them. But these mountains were so beautiful that he didn't even think about how it would feel to drive a piton in them with a hammer.

Up ahead they saw a yellow BMW pulled to the shoulder and a tall red-haired girl sitting on the bumper. She waved her arms at them.

"We should stop," Jonah yelled over the music.

"No way," Hamilton said. "We're on a Cahill mission."

"We have time to give her a lift to the next gas station," Jonah said. "C'mon, Ham — she's a damsel in distress. Where's your Samaritan spirit?"

"I don't think —" Hamilton started, but Jonah was already crossing a lane of traffic and pulling over.

The girl slid off the bumper as they came closer. Her jeans were tucked into soft leather boots. Her sweater fell alluringly off one shoulder. Hamilton gulped. Her hair, skin, and teeth were perfect. Her eyes were a vivid green.

"Nice ride," Jonah remarked. He paused, as though waiting for the girl to recognize him.

"Eet would be nicer if it had *le gas*," the girl said in a French accent. "I'm on my way to Salzburg for a shoot." Her gaze flickered past Jonah, and Hamilton saw surprise on his face that she didn't instantly recognize him.

"Shooting what?" Hamilton asked. "Ducks?"

"A tire catalog." She shrugged. "Not so exciting. But eet pays the bills when you're a model."

"You're a model? Never would have guessed," Jonah said in a lazy, teasing voice that caused Hamilton's head to swivel. He'd never seen Jonah flirt before.

The girl tilted her head. The glossy hair spilled down one bare shoulder. *"Un moment . . .* you look familiar."

Jonah grinned. "Yeah?"

"'Ave we met?" Are you an 'airdresser?"

"A *hairdresser*?" Jonah choked out.

"Guys, we'd better get going," Hamilton said.

"The name is Jonah," Jonah said, pronouncing his name carefully. He waited for a sign of recognition.

"Nicole."

"Jonah *Wizard."*

Nicole squinted at him. "You are a *wee-zhard?* Like the Harry Potter, *non*?"

"I'm Hamilton," Hamilton said, even though nobody asked.

Nicole looked at her watch. "I am so very late now!"

"Let's bounce," Jonah said. "We'll give you a ride to the next gas station. So, where are you from, Nicole? I've been all over France."

"I am from Paris."

"Score! They love your boy in Paris!"

Jonah trailed after Nicole, who leaned against the bumper to apply lipstick. Hamilton scooped up Nicole's heavy suitcase from her open trunk. He slammed the trunk shut and trudged back toward the car. Nicole was checking it out, circling around it with little coos of admiration. She ran her hand along the fender. "Eet is so *formidable,* zees car."

"Why don't you get into the backseat, Hamilton?"

Jonah suggested. "Nicole, do you like music? Are you a hip-hop fan?"

"I like *la musique, oui*," Nicole said. "*Le jazz.*"

"I can be mad jazzy," Jonah said.

Hamilton was stuffed into the tiny backseat with Nicole's suitcase. Even her purse was too big for the front seat. Instead, it sat on his lap.

A bee buzzed into the open window of the car, and, without pausing in her conversation with Jonah, Nicole grabbed it in its midair flight. She crushed it in her fist, then flicked the carcass out the window.

Whoa, Hamilton thought. Even models could have amazing reflexes.

"Tell me the story of your life and I'll tell you mine," Jonah said to Nicole. "But first, are you sure you don't recognize me?"

"Is this place real?" Dan asked, looking up at King Ludwig's castle. "Or am I in Disneyland?"

Up the winding trail through the pines loomed the castle, a folly built by a mad king, all turrets and windows and gables and peaked roofs and windows winking back in the slowly sliding sun. The castle was situated on a high, rocky cliff, with snow-capped Alpine mountains rising around it. It overlooked a sparkling, deep blue lake. Isolated and yet proud of its grandeur, this castle flaunted the crazy.

The Nazis had crammed millions of dollars of looted

treasure in that magnificent castle. Jane Sperling had come in 1945, maybe on a misty day like this one. She'd found her old enemy here. Amy was sure of it.

"Actually, the castle was used as the model for Sleeping Beauty's Castle in Disneyland," she said. She checked her cell phone again, but there were no messages. No calls. "Where *are* they?"

She'd left messages for both Jonah and Hamilton. They hadn't checked in with Attleboro, either. She was starting to worry.

She punched in the Attleboro number. "Are you having any problems with *Gideon*?" she asked. "We still haven't heard from Jonah and Hamilton."

"Satellite in the mountains can be iffy, even for the *Gideon*," Evan reassured her. "Give them more time."

"Did the GPS map come through?" Ian asked.

"Check," Dan said, glancing at his wrist. "I've got a bead on a room down in the tunnels."

"That's the room where the ERR kept its records," Ian said. "We think you should start there. That would have been the first place Jane would have gone to look for evidence of the de Virga."

"If they don't show up in twenty minutes, we're going in without them," Amy said.

"Let's hope it doesn't come to that," Ian put in. "Just fridge yourselves, as Jonah says."

"Dude," Dan said. "Do you mean *chill*?"

"Precisely. Just what I said."

"Give me the phone, Ian." Evan took the phone off

speaker. "Listen, I know it's hard to wait. But I don't like you going in without backup."

"I'll give them ten more minutes," Amy said.

"I've got a stubborn girlfriend."

"You're just realizing that, huh."

Amy cut the connection and drew her jacket closer around her. It was cool under the pines. Dan sat on the side of the road, leaning against his pack and drinking one of the six-pack of soda he'd bought in the village. Amy could picture Evan's half smile, the way his mouth curved on one end. It was as though she could *feel* it, the warmth in his eyes when he looked at her.

Just then she felt a buzzing in her jacket pocket. Vesper One. She signaled to Dan.

```
Sightseeing? The Alps are so lovely this
time of year. But don't forget I'm waiting
for the arrival of the next package! If
you need some incentive, I've got seven
ideas. Just let me know!


Vesper One
```

"Another threat," Dan said.

They both turned to face the castle above them on the mountain. The sun had dropped behind the tall pines, and shadows stretched toward them.

"We can't wait any longer for backup," Amy said. "We've got to go in."

CHAPTER 15

Jonah didn't know how it had happened. He only knew that they were lost. The GPS had stopped working. They'd had to get off the autobahn. Nicole had directed them to an exit, since the GPS was still working on her phone. But after twenty minutes of driving past farms and cows, Jonah was beginning to suspect that Nicole was not what she seemed.

He checked her out again. There was something about her . . .

The clouds cleared, and a bright shaft of sunlight illuminated the curve of her cheek. Jonah tried not to stare. He was an actor, and he knew makeup. There was a telltale line along the bridge of her nose. And did perfect girls sweat along their hairlines?

They do if they're wearing wigs. He met Hamilton's eyes in the rearview mirror. He cut his eyes over to Nicole. Hamilton nodded. He knew something was off, too.

Oldest trick in the book. And he'd fallen for it.

"Ze gas station ees just around thees bend," Nicole said. "I zink. . . ."

"Why don't you let Hamilton take a look at your phone?" Jonah suggested. Again his eyes flicked to Hamilton's.

"Let me check it out," Hamilton said. "I'm totally good at GPS." He leaned forward and put his meaty hand on her phone. She tried to keep it, but Hamilton's grip was not to be denied. With a slight hiss through her teeth, she let go.

Jonah made the right turn. He pulled the wheel hard, and she put out a hand to steady herself. He caught a glimpse of a tattoo on the inside of her wrist. A purple triceratops—just like her brother.

He almost groaned out loud. How could he have been such an idiot? He'd seen the photo of Cheyenne Wyoming. But this girl looked nothing like her.

Because, you fool, she's wearing a wig, a fake nose, and contact lenses!

"I can't get the GPS to work on this thing," Hamilton said, looking at the phone.

"May I 'ave it back?" Cheyenne put her hand over it and yanked it.

They needed to ditch her, and fast. Who knew what she was planning?

"Look, there's a farmer!" he called.

"'Ee is way out in ze field," Cheyenne said.

It was true. The man was a dot in the grass, and the stone wall in front was at least six feet high.

"It's the best we can do," Jonah said, jerking the wheel.

The car skidded to a stop. "Hmm," Jonah said. "Girls are so much better at charming directions out of cranky farmers."

"Totally!" Hamilton jumped out and then opened Cheyenne's door. He practically lifted her out.

"I cannot climb zat wall!"

"No problemo," Hamilton said. He picked her up, and, as she shrieked, lifted her onto the wall.

Hamilton quickly jogged back to the car and squeezed into the front seat.

"Punch it!" he yelled.

Gravel flew as the car skidded back onto the road.

"That was crazy!" Jonah said, pounding the wheel. "I can't believe we were so stupid! That was Cheyenne Wyoming!"

"*We* were stupid, dude? You're the one who said let's pick her up!"

"Dawg, that's a low blow." But he knew Hamilton was right.

"She completely hosed us," Hamilton said. "I think she blocked our satellite signal. She must have planted some sort of device in the car." He began to search along the dashboard and floor, looking for a blocker. "You were probably too busy trying to get her to recognize you to notice. At least I got her phone."

"Whoa! How did you manage that? I saw her take it back, bro!"

"Last summer, at the mansion? Dan and I took lessons from Lightfinger Larry."

Hamilton accessed the phone. "I'm going to check her old messages. . . . She has a text! 'G is in the picture. Could need removal—'"

Hamilton stared at the screen as the letters began to disappear. "It's getting wiped! I can't read the rest!"

"The phone is probably password-protected to erase," Jonah said. "Chill, bro. Attleboro might be able to put some spyware on it."

Hamilton looked over at him nervously. "But why was she trying to delay us? Do you think Casper is up there with Amy and Dan?"

Jonah pressed the accelerator down. "Let's just hope Amy and Dan wait for us before they go in."

Amy and Dan had toured the courtyard and pretended to admire the splendid panorama of lake and mountains with the other tourists. They'd shuffled through the imposing rooms that opened one after another in grand magnificence: the throne room, the study room, and the drawing room. They had tilted their heads back pretending to admire the elaborate murals that portrayed scenes from Ludwig's favorite operas. They had circled around, trying to figure out how to get away without the guide noticing them. But the rooms were too large, and the crowd was too small.

"We just have to do it," Amy whispered. "This place is so big they'll never know where we went. And we'll be in the tunnels . . . they won't think of looking there."

"All right. As soon as the guide starts to talk again, fade back."

The guide turned toward a mural and started to talk about a Wagner opera. Dan figured it was the perfect opportunity to go, or else he'd pass out from boredom.

They backed away behind a red curtain, made their way to a doorway, and stepped through. They were in a long hallway, and they quickly ran down it. Dan checked his GPS watch and put the earpiece in his ear.

"Left, then right."

They were in a part of the castle that was closed to visitors. Dan led them down the back staircase and past the vast kitchen. From there they found the door that led to the lower levels and the tunnels. Amy was expecting small, cramped, and dirty spaces, but the tunnels were large and airy. They could see a group of tourists just exiting out to the courtyard.

Dan kept moving, listening to the instructions in his earpiece. They followed turn after turn. Finally, he stopped.

"This is the one," Dan said. He removed the earpiece and pushed open the door.

The room was completely empty except for a battered gray filing cabinet. They opened the drawers, but they were empty.

"Talk to me, Jane." Amy slammed the drawer shut. "Where did you leave it?"

Dan began to run his hands along the bricks on the

far wall. He followed the line of bricks that met the floor. Nothing.

"The floor slopes," Amy said suddenly. "Why is that?"

"Well, it's a tunnel," Dan said. "It could flood. There's probably a drain."

Amy followed the slope of the floor and found a tiny square drain.

"Dan!" she cried. "In the article I read, Jane said '*All down the drain*'!"

Dan peered down at the drain. "You think?"

"I think. Can you get the grating off?"

Dan got out his multi-tool and fitted the blade against the drain. It took him several minutes, but he was able to pop it free.

Taking a breath, Amy reached her hand in. She felt along a corroded pipe. "Yuck," she said. She lay down on the floor, her cheek against the cold stone, and stretched her arm as far as she could.

"There's something here," she said, her heart beating. "A string . . . looped around something . . ."

"Can you get it?"

"I think so. . . ." Slowly, painstakingly, Amy drew up a small, flat package wrapped in yellowed plastic. Her hands shook as she carefully unwrapped it.

A small black leather notebook was revealed. Not the de Virga map. Disappointed, Amy carefully opened the flap of the notebook with a fingertip.

Written in faded pen she saw initials on the inside front cover: *JS june1945.*

"Jane," Amy breathed.

She gently turned the page. Written in pencil, so faint she could hardly read it, was:

TO G: DV528.112K

STOLEN BY HUMMEL

REPATRIATED W V. KEPLER

RESTING W/ TEACHER & VICTIM

TOGETHER WITH THE
SPELLBOUND WANDERER
WILL POINT THE WAY

"Oh, terrific," Dan muttered. "Just what we need! Another code! Why can't people just say what they mean? Why can't they say THE MAP IS IN THE DESK?"

Amy quickly thumbed through the notebook. The rest of the pages were empty. "At least we found something that will lead us to it." Amy slipped the notebook into the inner pocket of her jacket. "Now let's get out of here. I have a creepy feeling about this place."

"Hmmm. Secret passageways, tunnels, Nazi ghosts, security, a mad king . . . I have no idea what you mean."

"Going so fast? But you forgot something."

The voice echoed outside in the tunnel. Amy and Dan jerked up from where they were kneeling as a figure blocked the doorway.

"Me."

It was Casper Wyoming. He leaned against the doorway, a glittering knife in his hand.

The road climbed into the mountains, Jonah taking the hairpin curves as fast as he dared.

"You look so macho clutching the door handle that way," he said to Hamilton.

"Just . . . be . . . careful," Hamilton said through clenched teeth.

Ahead Jonah could see a particularly winding set of turns that led to a spindly looking bridge over a gorge. He eased off the accelerator. He wanted speed, but he wasn't suicidal.

He hit the brakes for the first curve. The car didn't slow but scraped against the guardrail.

"WHOA!" Hamilton shouted, looking down into the gorge. "Dude, the brake pedal is on the left!"

With an uneasy feeling, Jonah pumped the brakes. The pedal went to the floor. His hands were suddenly sweaty on the wheel. "There's something wrong with the brakes." He didn't recognize his shaky, weak voice. He pumped them again. Nothing.

"There's something wrong with the BRAKES?"

"I don't think we have any."

"We don't have any BRAKES?"

"Bro, it doesn't help to repeat everything I say!" Jonah yelled.

"She did it!" Hamilton cried. "She planted some kind of device. . . ."

Jonah downshifted as the car roared up the mountain. The engine protested in an angry whine. "C'mon, baby, work with me!"

At least they were climbing now. The natural drag was slowing down the car.

"It must be remote-activated or something. . . . Watch OUT!" Hamilton screamed, as another curve loomed ahead. Jonah barely made it, tires squealing. "Or maybe it's inside the car and I can find it!" Frantically, Hamilton began to search.

Jonah concentrated on the car. "Keep your seat belt on! And secure any loose items in the car." If they went over the side, anything that flew in the air would turn into a missile.

"Maybe it's in her suitcase!" Hamilton twisted in his seat. He undid his seat belt and reached behind, grabbing Cheyenne's big purse and flinging it out the window. Then he wrestled with her suitcase and forced it through the small space. He tried not to look as the suitcase bounced and careened off the side of the mountain, splitting in two. That could be him in a minute.

"Check the brakes!" he yelled. He stuffed himself back into the seat and clicked the seat belt shut.

A perspiring Jonah shook his head. "Sorry, bro. That wasn't it."

Jonah was using the shift to brake now, remembering his driving course. He had been taught how to use steering to control the car, how to accelerate into curves and keep the car on the road. He tried to remember everything he'd learned about downshifting, about the process of deceleration and acceleration. . . .

He just wished his hands weren't sweating so badly. . . .

"The bridge." Hamilton's normally deep voice was a squeak. "If you don't make that turn, we'll go straight off."

Jonah didn't answer. There was no answer. Hamilton was right.

He tried to plan the route even as he struggled to keep the car on the road. He would need to come out of that turn and downshift immediately. He could see from here that it was impossible. Unless . . . unless he used the side of the mountain to slow down the car. Just enough so that he wouldn't lose control . . .

He swallowed and gripped the wheel.

"Hang on," he tried to say, but his mouth was so dry the words barely made it out.

He eased the car to the left.

"What are you doing?" Hamilton yelled.

The car slammed against the mountain and then jerked back on the road. That didn't work. Too hard.

He eased it over again, this time watching carefully. The side mirror snapped off. Sparks flew. The car was slowing, definitely . . . but he was heading for the curve.

He bumped back on the road, the wheel shuddering in his hands. He took the curve on two wheels. For an instant, the clear Alpine air was all they saw, dark blue sky and dark green pines. . . .

The car shivered and kept the road. Jonah downshifted, fighting gravity, fighting the road, fighting the mountain, fighting the VESPERS, because he was going to WIN. . . .

The car straightened out and zoomed over the bridge. Jonah kept it steady.

"Jonah! Up ahead, on the left—that road. See it? It's going uphill."

Jonah saw what Hamilton meant. If he could make that turn, the car would naturally slow as it climbed the mountain. If he stayed straight, they'd be traveling down the mountain again. With more curves to navigate, more chances to crash . . .

It was their only hope.

Below them was a thousand feet of air. The bridge was narrow. He wouldn't have room to swing out to the right. He'd have to make it—or go spinning out, crash through a guardrail and leap straight into space.

CHAPTER 16

Now!

Jonah pulled the wheel to the left and the car responded, going airborne for a moment as it bumped off the road, hit a rail, then landed on the uphill road. Jonah steered and downshifted all the way up the road until he was able to gently crash into a rock on the shoulder.

The car stopped. His head hit the wheel. Hamilton crashed against the dashboard.

"Oh, dawg," Hamilton said.

"Oh, dude," Jonah said.

"That was close. That was so close to close, it was almost over."

"As close to a final destination as I ever want to get," Jonah said.

With shaking hands, they dug out their cell phones and backpacks. As soon as they stepped out of the car, the cell phones began to work. Amy didn't pick up. Neither did Dan. Attleboro hadn't heard from them in the past thirty minutes.

"We've got to get to them!" Hamilton said. He slammed his fist on the car.

"Dude, it's a rental. Do you have to dent it, too?" Jonah crouched by the car. "We just need to find the device so Attleboro can check on it. It could be a lead." He held up a small ball. "This baby is a videocam. That's how she knew when to blow the brakes for maximum impact."

They grabbed their gear and half ran, half slid down to the road. It was empty.

Hamilton threw his pack on the ground and let out a howl of frustration.

"Wait. I hear something," Jonah said.

They exchanged a glance. What if it was Cheyenne? What if she'd met up with some other Vesper bad dudes? Suddenly, the road felt isolated, and they felt exposed.

A dot appeared across the divide, taking the last turn for the bridge. The dot turned into a minibus as it crossed the bridge and headed toward them. No matter how jangled their nerves, a minibus seemed like a good sign. Jonah stepped out into the road, waving his arms. Hamilton tensed, ready to attack if he had to.

The minibus screeched to a halt. A young woman with blond braids stuck her head out the window.

"Jonah WIZARD!" she screamed.

Casper took out a large red apple. He began to peel

it with the knife. It was mesmerizing, watching the bright, polished silver blade move around the apple. An impossibly thin strip of peel began to spiral downward.

"Hey, guys," Casper said. "I missed you."

Dread invaded Amy's bones, and she didn't think she could move. He was blocking the doorway, and they were trapped. She didn't want to go anywhere near that glittering knife.

"The last time we were together, I was deep in a crevasse next to a dead guy," Casper said. "And you didn't even say good-bye."

The peel slowly fell to the floor. Casper carved out a piece of apple with a few flicks of the knife. He did it so quickly and expertly that Amy shuddered.

He held out the piece of apple on the tip of the knife. "Anybody? No?" He sucked it off the knife. If he was trying to unnerve them, it was working.

"What is it, Casper?" Amy hated that her voice shook. "What do you want?"

"Oh, didn't I say? The map. I want the map."

"We don't have the map. And we still have another three days to produce it."

"But you found something. I heard you." Casper sliced off another piece of apple, flicked it into his mouth, and crunched down on it.

"You have to allow us to follow the clues," Amy said. "That's the deal."

Casper smiled. He flicked a piece of apple at Amy. It hit her in the face. She flinched. "I didn't make any deal, sunshine."

He took another step closer and flicked another piece of apple at Amy. It struck her on the cheek. Dan clenched his fists together.

"'At least we found something that will lead us to it.'" Casper mimicked Amy's soft, high voice, then snorted and tossed his apple away. "You think you two are the only smart people in the world? You said you found something that will *lead you to it*. So hand it over, sunshine, or else!"

"Or else what?" Dan asked. "You'll kill us? Your boss won't be happy."

"I don't have to kill both of you." Casper smiled. "Just one will do."

Amy's legs were shaking so badly she was afraid she'd fall down. She reached out to hold Dan's arm. If she couldn't find the strength to protect herself, she knew she'd protect her brother.

"What difference does it make, Ames?" Dan asked. "He's a Vesper. Why shouldn't we give it to him?" He stooped down for his backpack.

Dan was reaching for his pack, but Amy had the notebook in her pocket. What was Dan planning?

"No funny business," Casper warned.

"Dude, if you think I care which Vesper gets this, you're crazy."

Amy was braced for anything, but Dan's move surprised even her. He came up with the full can of soda in his hand and hurled it straight at Casper. It slammed him in the forehead. There was an almost comical look of stunned surprise on his face before Amy gathered her nerve and followed Dan's move with a flying martial-arts kick at the hand holding the knife.

The knife skittered along the floor. Dan whirled and kicked it into the drain.

Casper screamed a curse. Dan bashed him in the head with his backpack. They heard a thud as the soda cans connected with his skull. Casper staggered.

They shouldered past him and raced out into the tunnel.

Amy thought frantically. She knew the tunnel would eventually lead outside to the courtyard. What they needed was a crowd. But if a tour wasn't leaving, the courtyard could be empty.

"Which way to the upstairs?" she asked Dan.

"I don't know!" he shouted.

They heard running footsteps behind them, and they knew Casper had recovered.

"I hear something," she gasped out. "Listen!"

Ludwig was mad, bro

But he also was bad, bro

Was his own 'Iliad,' bro . . ."

"Jonah!" Amy breathed. Where there was Jonah, there would be a crowd.

Ahead of them, Casper suddenly appeared from around a bend. He must have found a way around them. He lifted a hand and snapped open another knife. And smiled.

They stopped. From off to the right, Amy could hear Jonah's voice. But it was *fading*, not getting louder.

"Before, I was annoyed," Casper said. "Now, I'm mad."

Amy took a deep breath. "OMIGOSH JONAH WIZARD!" she squealed. Just like millions of girls shrieked all over the world. The sound bounced off the walls of the tunnel.

Casper looked at her as though she'd lost her mind.

It only took a moment before they heard Jonah's voice. Coming *closer*. And fast.

"NEVER WORE PLAID, BRO!"

Amy almost wept in relief.

Jonah burst into the main tunnel at a run, surrounded by a crowd of giggling girls. Castle security flanked them. Hamilton hurried up to them. He followed Amy's gaze and saw Casper. His fists tightened at his side.

Casper surveyed the crowd. His gaze lingered on Hamilton's fists, the security officers, the way Jonah moved, pushing the crowd so that it would squeeze Casper against the wall. He stepped off to the side as the crowd rushed by, Amy and Dan safely in its midst.

As they passed him, he drew his finger across his neck in a classic "you're dead" signal and pointed at them.

"Later," he mouthed.

CHAPTER 17

The sunset was spectacular, and they were safe in the minibus with the students from Estonia who were on their way to Salzburg for the *Sound of Music* tour. Jonah sat up front with the girls and led a sing-along.

Who would have guessed that the hip-hop star knew all the words to "Climb Ev'ry Mountain"?

Amy, Dan, and Hamilton huddled in the back of the bus.

"Why would Casper and Cheyenne want to kill us?" Amy asked. "It doesn't make sense. Why go to all the trouble of kidnapping Cahills and getting us to help if they're going to kill us before we finish?"

"Maybe Vesper One doesn't know about it," Hamilton said. "Maybe they're going rogue. Like they want to impress him or something. It's the kind of thing my sisters would do," he added sheepishly.

Amy and Dan stared at him.

"I mean, what do I know?" he said, shifting uncomfortably. "Nothing, right?"

"No, that's brilliant," Dan said.

Amy nodded. "The only problem is, we have no way of telling Vesper One."

"And they're probably counting on that," Dan said.

"Great," Amy said. "Now we've got the Wyomings as well as Interpol breathing down our necks. And time's running out to find the map."

"I'm going to check with Attleboro," Hamilton said. He scooted away and took out his phone. They had already sent Jane's notation to Massachusetts.

"You were great in there," Amy told Dan. "When I saw Casper, I couldn't move."

"You kicked that knife out of his hand."

"Only because you nailed him so hard with that can." Amy bit her lip. "I was so scared, Dan. I couldn't think." She shook her head. "I feel so ashamed of myself. If it wasn't for you, we would have been toast."

"Whoa," Dan said. "If you're throwing a pity party for yourself, don't invite me." He poked her. "You were the one who got Jonah to find us. Awesome lung power. I thought you only used that volume to get me out of the bathroom."

Amy smiled, but the heaviness was still in her heart. She looked out at the dark mountains. They seemed to be pressing against them. "But what if the day comes when we don't figure it out? When—"

"We are not going to lose." Dan's gaze was fierce. "I remember what Nellie looked like on that video. And Fiske, and Phoenix, and Ted, and all of them. And we are not going to lose. *No matter what.*"

Amy should have felt comforted. But there was something about Dan's confidence . . . what was it?

It wasn't confidence. It was more like desperation.

Hamilton slid back into the seat. "They have a lead for us. Look."

THE V WITH KEPLER HUNG US UP FOR A BIT. IT MUST STAND FOR VESPER. IF THE WORLD-FAMOUS SEVENTEENTH-CENTURY ASTRONOMER JOHANNES KEPLER WAS A VESPER.

Amy quickly typed in a response:

WAS A MANUSCRIPT BY KEPLER STOLEN BY NAZIS?

YES. EARLY COPY OF MYSTERIUM COSMOGRAPHICUM. WAS HELD AT NEUSCHWANSTEIN CASTLE. BOOK NOW IN POSSESSION OF LIBRARY OF PHILOSOPHY AND COSMOLOGY IN PRAGUE.

"That means that Jane could have found a record of it in the castle," Amy said. "*Repatriated* means 'returned to the country of origin.' So maybe she slipped the de Virga in with the Kepler book? I don't know what 'resting with teacher and victim' means . . . yet. But she's trying to tell us something."

Dan nodded. "And that means we're going to Prague."

Prague, Czech Republic

The Library of Philosophy and Cosmology had existed in Prague for four hundred years. Originally attached to a monastery, it was now housed in an ultramodern building designed by a world-famous architect who was fond of using stainless steel like ribbon candy. Dan didn't know whether to enter the library or take a bite out of it.

They walked inside a paneled foyer that held only a polished-steel umbrella stand. It was empty. "Remember, we're Sarah and Jack Teague," Amy murmured. "The Farleys are history."

Glass doors swung open as they walked forward. A curved desk of dark polished wood was ahead of them. Through glass doors they could see the great reading room of the library, shelves rising to a second-level gallery. Long tables ran the width of the room. Only a few people were scattered around, heads bent over books and laptops.

The woman sitting at the desk looked up from her computer. She wore glasses with heavy black frames that somehow made her look cool instead of nerdy. Shiny black hair was scraped back in a tight ponytail.

"May I help you?"

"We're American students," Amy said. "We'd like to look something up in your library." She smiled, trying to ingratiate herself.

"Do you have a letter of reference?"

"No," Amy said.

"This is a private library," the woman said. "For invited scholars only. I'm sorry. There are other libraries in Prague that would be able to accommodate you, I'm sure." She turned back to her computer.

"But . . ." Amy started. She desperately tried to think. How could she bluff their way in? "This is the only library that can help us."

"Can you tell me the subject of your research?"

"Uh, the early books of Johannes Kepler."

"We have only one."

"We know," Dan said. "The one that was rescued from Neuschwanstein Castle at the end of the war."

She pressed her lips together. "That is one of our most valuable books. We cannot allow just anyone to handle it."

"Is there somebody else we can speak to? The director, perhaps?" Amy asked politely.

"I am Katja Mavel, the director of the library. I am afraid I am your last resort."

"My sister and I are students of Dr. Mark Rosenbloom," Dan blurted.

Amy tried not to look surprised. Mark Rosenbloom was the father of Jake and Atticus, the boys who had turned them in to Interpol. Sure, he was a world-famous archaeologist, but they'd never met him.

The woman paused. "Dr. Rosenbloom referred you?"

"Yes, but we misplaced the letter."

"Perhaps you should e-mail Dr. Rosenbloom and then he can forward the necessary papers."

"We can't," Dan said. "He's on a dig in . . . Eritrea. No satellite reception."

Amy glanced at her brother. Where had that come from? She didn't even think he could locate Eritrea on a map. She didn't think *she* could. But suddenly Dan was projecting maturity and intelligence. How did he manage it? And why couldn't he do this at the dinner table instead of using his spoon to catapult mashed potatoes onto her plate when she asked for seconds?

The woman seemed hesitant, but her tone was firm. "I am so sorry, but we cannot make exceptions. I've met Dr. Rosenbloom and I know of his work. But I cannot let you in without the necessary papers." Her voice softened. "I'm sure there is a way to contact him. Perhaps he could call in the introduction for you. We can bend the rules, but we cannot break them. Good day."

Amy quickly scribbled a secure e-mail address on a piece of paper and the name *Sarah Teague*. "If we get Dr. Rosenbloom to e-mail you, can you e-mail us back that you'll admit us?"

"I can't make any promises." Dr. Mavel glanced at the paper. She didn't say yes, but she tucked it into a drawer.

There was nothing to do but leave. Amy and Dan stood on the sidewalk outside the library. It was a lovely fall day, cool and crisp. The city of Prague, with its old, graceful buildings, its hills and steeples, spread out around them. They could see the Vltava River and Prague Castle. But Amy couldn't take it in. She could almost feel time passing, like the wind that blew her hair back and scattered the leaves at her feet.

"I don't know what to do now," she said. "But it was a good idea to bring up Atticus's father."

"It still didn't get us in. And it's not like we can call him. Jake probably told him that we're thieves."

Amy remembered the look on Jake's face, the contempt when he knew what they were planning. "We'll have to put out a Cahill alert," she decided. "Someone will come through. In the meantime we can focus on getting a good translation of the epilogue of *Il Milione*. It has to tie in with everything else somehow."

"Pliny the Younger, Marco Polo, Caravaggio, Johannes Kepler, and a Nazi," Dan said, ticking off the names on his fingers. "They're all centuries apart, and they're connected?"

"They've got to be," Amy said. "Let's head back to the hotel."

They had checked in to a small hotel tucked away on a side street upon their arrival that morning. The room hadn't been ready, and they were carrying around their packs, which were starting to feel heavy. Jonah and Hamilton had gone to a four-star American hotel. They had agreed it would be safer to split up.

As they trudged the blocks to the hotel, Dan could feel the weight of discouragement even more than the drag of the pack on his shoulders. He pictured Hamilton and Jonah sitting around their hotel room in plush robes, nibbling at a complimentary fruit basket.

As they entered the hotel, the clerk came around the desk to speak to them. "My apologies. Your room isn't ready," he said. "May I suggest a snack in the *kavarna* — the café. Complimentary, of course."

"Dude," Dan said. "You just said the magic word."

They were tired of walking. Tired of thinking. A little pastry sugar rush would do them good.

They headed for the café adjoining the lobby, where they sat down at a table and ordered hot chocolate and *vdolek*, a pastry with jam and whipped cream.

Dan was just about to dip his spoon into the pastry when Amy stiffened. The same hawk-nosed man who'd been on the train to Lucerne pushed through the door of the hotel.

"Dan!"

Dan licked his lips as he regarded his pastry. "This looks like a cloud of paradise."

The man went directly to the desk.

Interpol.

Amy ducked behind the broad back of a patron enjoying a large plate of pastries.

Don't tell him where we are. Don't tell him don't tell him don't tell him.

The clerk looked at the paper the man held out. He pointed to the café.

CHAPTER 18

"We have to get out of here." Amy stood. "Now."

"Wait! My *vdolek*!" Dan protested, reaching for it.

She yanked on his arm just as he grabbed for it. Dan went facedown in the whipped cream.

She bent over as though to pick up a purse. In the mirror over the counter she could clearly see the Interpol detective trying to peer into the café. All he saw was a boy with a faceful of whipped cream.

Dan reached for a napkin, but she shoved the pastry up against his face again.

"*Mmff!*" Dan protested around a mouthful of cream.

Keeping his back to the lobby, she steered them through the door. Outside, she pushed Dan forward until they were swallowed by a crowd of tourists.

Dan swiped at the whipped cream on his face and licked his fingers as they weaved through the crowd. "Escape was never so sweet," he crowed.

The package arrived that afternoon. Sinead had immediately taken it upstairs to the comm. center. Cheyenne's phone had certainly been wiped clean, but that didn't mean they couldn't get some information out of it. She got to work.

Ian researched the videocam Cheyenne had stuck on the car fender. It was so micro and advanced that, like the DeOssie smartphone, it had to come from military or spy agencies. If he cross-referenced with the names that were starting to come in on the DeOssie . . . maybe they could find a connection.

Evan and Sinead had written a program to research the jacket label they'd gotten off the video from Vesper One. It was a company in the Czech Republic with factories in China that sold throughout the US and Europe. With a new expanded search engine, the computer was now pulling up every retail outlet that carried the brand. It was a long list.

Ian checked the program over Evan's shoulder. He stared at the store names, which blurred in front of his tired eyes.

"What is Walmart?" he asked.

"It's the newest luxury store. Just like Harrod's. You'd love it," Evan assured him.

"Whoa!" Sinead suddenly leaped to her feet. "Bingo! That last text for Cheyenne? I've tracked down the location! You are not going to believe this!"

Amy felt her cell buzz in her pocket. She plucked it out. There was a text from Sinead.

URGENT! TRACED ORIGIN OF LAST TEXT ON CHEYENNE'S PHONE. WAS SENT FROM TOWN OF KUTNÁ HORA — CLOSE TO PRAGUE. CONTACT ATTLEBORO IMMEDIATELY.

It was a breakthrough. A real breakthrough.

Amy showed Dan the text. "That's three connections to the Czech Republic — Jane's note, the jacket label, and now the text! Maybe the hostages are being held right near here!"

They turned off the main street onto a quiet side street. Amy quickly dialed Attleboro and put Dan on three-way calling.

"There you are!" Sinead let out an explosive sigh of relief. "Did you get my text?"

"Great news! Where's Kutná Hora?"

"It's only about forty minutes from Prague. We've been able to pinpoint the exact location — it was actually sent from Sedlec, a suburb of Kutná Hora. There's a church there called All Saints — we think it was sent from there."

"What did the text say?"

"We couldn't retrieve it," Sinead said, disappointed. "We only know what Hamilton saw—"

"'G is in the picture, could need removal,'" Amy

repeated from memory. "Jane mentions a 'G,' too. But it can't be the same one. There are so many random pieces in this puzzle!"

"Tell me about it," Sinead said. "Erasmus is on his way to Rome to see Mr. McIntyre. They're going to brainstorm ways to get Interpol off your back. Maybe pull some strings. And Ian is working on a Cahill connection to get you in at the library."

"Great. We'll leave for Kutná Hora right now."

"Look, we just want you to check it out. Surveillance only. If you suspect the hostages are there, hang back. Don't do anything crazy. We can put a team together in twenty-four hours if we need to."

"But if we wait, they could be moved! What would *you* do?" Amy waited out the pause. Sinead was her best friend. She knew that Sinead would want to protect her. But she'd also tell her the truth.

"I'd go in," Sinead said.

Rome, Italy

The apartment felt lonely now that their father was away, and in the morning Atticus and Jake Rosenbloom began a new routine of flopping on the deep couches in their dad's study to do their work. Surrounded by their father's books and stacks of files, they felt closer to him.

Atticus could tell that his half brother, Jake, was still brooding about what had happened with Amy and

Dan Cahill. Jake had turned them in to Interpol, but the authorities didn't seem to believe Jake when he'd said they'd stolen the original manuscript of Marco Polo's *Il Milione*.

Atticus was getting over his shock and hurt. He'd thought and thought about it, and he'd decided that there must be something going on that Dan was afraid to tell him. They were buddies, even though Dan was two years older. He still remembered the look on Dan's face as he seized *Il Milione* and took off. Like he'd wanted to tell Atticus something, but he couldn't.

He'd felt so let down by Dan, but he didn't have many friends to spare. Being an eleven-year-old college freshman wasn't easy. He couldn't exactly join in conversations about dating or concerts. And he didn't have much to say to kids his own age, either. They just thought he was weird. Atticus smiled, remembering what Dan's response to Atticus saying that had been. *Dude, you* are *weird. Embrace the weirdness! It's cool.*

"What do you want for breakfast" Jake asked him.

"Are you actually going to cook?" Atticus asked.

"I think I can manage to boil water and put some oatmeal in it."

Atticus snorted. "If you think that's all there is to it, you haven't lived in Italy long enough."

The phone rang, and both brothers looked at it for a moment before bending over their books again. Mark Rosenbloom was a world-famous scholar with a bestselling book. He got calls all the time.

The answering machine was turned up, and the accented voice was clear and crisp.

"Good afternoon, Dr. Rosenbloom."

"Hungarian," Jake said.

"Czech," Atticus corrected. Jake was terrible at accents.

"This is Katja Mavel, from the Library of Philosophy and Cosmology in Prague. Perhaps . . . ah . . . you'll remember me from your last visit." The voice had suddenly dropped in a flirtatious way.

Jake rolled his eyes. Atticus sighed. Sometimes it was hard being a skinny nerd with glasses in the Rosenbloom family. Mark Rosenbloom tended to make librarians weak in the knees. Jake had inherited every bit of his dark good looks.

"We shared a cup of coffee and you were *zo* informative about cataloging our object collection. . . ."

With a sigh, Atticus got up to turn off the volume on the machine.

"In any event, I thought I would contact you directly about two students of yours who say you sent them to us. A brother and a sister. They looked rather young . . . but I know that you do work with younger students. Perhaps they are prodigies like your son."

Atticus stopped. Jake sat up.

"Sarah Teague, she said her name was. They said they were researching Johannes Kepler? The *Mysterium Cosmographicum*—the one that was rescued from

Neuschwanstein Castle after the war. Odd, because I did not think this was quite your field. We could not let them in without the proper letters of introduction. I am *zo* sorry if this becomes a problem. If you could call me directly, I'm sure we would be able to clear this up. Good-bye, Dr. Rosenbloom . . . Mark."

Jake threw aside his book. "It's them! It's those Cahills!"

"We don't know that for sure," Atticus said.

"Of course it is. Stop protecting him!" Jake fumed. "Now they're probably using our father's name and reputation to steal something else!"

"You don't know that they're going to steal anything!"

"Atticus, come on! They stole a priceless manuscript! They're crooks!"

"A thief doesn't say he's sorry. Dan said that to me! And he really meant it! He didn't *want* to take it."

Jake shook his head sadly. "Buddy, you've got to stop hero-worshipping this guy."

"I'm not!" Atticus's throat felt tight.

Jake stood up. "I'm going to call Interpol."

"They didn't believe you last time."

"This time I'll be more convincing." Jake crossed the room in three quick steps. "Who knows what they're going to steal next? The Mad King's body?!"

Atticus froze. "What did you say?"

"Neuschwanstein Castle. It was built by Ludwig

the Second. What you don't know about history after A.D. 100 scares me."

Atticus felt the words hit him like hard punches, like when he used to get beat up at his locker before his parents took him out of middle school.

Jake had his hand on the receiver. Atticus leaped across the room and threw himself at his brother. It was like a small twig battling a redwood. "You can't!"

"Hey!" Jake backed up. "What *is* it with you?"

"You can't," Atticus repeated desperately. How could he convince Jake not to call in the authorities? How could he tell him that everything had changed when he'd mentioned the Mad King?

Atticus's thoughts whirled. It couldn't be a coincidence. It just couldn't.

He squeezed his eyes shut for a moment as the memories lit up his brain. The night she died. A memory he always blocked, because the sight and sounds of her dying were so terrible he never wanted to revisit them.

Until he had to. Right here, right now.

That night, everyone else had gone from the hospital room where they had been sitting vigil for three days. Astrid had been sick for weeks with a mysterious illness the doctors could not identify. Suddenly, she had taken a turn for the worse. She'd collapsed at her office and had been rushed to the hospital. She hadn't regained consciousness.

Jake took their exhausted father to get coffee downstairs. Her devoted assistant, Dave, had finally listened when Mark told him to go home to bed. There was only Atticus in the room. He was hungry and tired, too, but they all knew that they couldn't bear to leave her alone. As though if they did, she would die.

She died anyway.

At first, he thought he was overhearing her dreams. *"V-One. He's V-One! Vespers . . ."*

Then she'd come fully awake. He was holding her hand when he felt his being squeezed.

"Mom!" Tears spurted into his eyes when he saw her smile.

"Atticus." She wet her lips. "So thirsty."

He gave her a sip of water. "I'll get Dad."

"No! You must listen. Last chance."

"You're going to get better." Atticus choked back tears.

She squeezed his hand. "Listen. Very carefully. Remember the bedtime story? The one I used to tell you?"

Atticus nodded. He didn't remember the story very well, not really, but he wanted her to calm down.

"The ring. The ring. Do you remember? They can help you. But they don't know who we are! I am passing along guardianship to you."

Guardianship? Of who? Jake? Jake was seven years older than he was. Of course, Atticus always told Jake he was way smarter, but he was joking. Half joking.

"You are a guardian. You must continue. Tradition. So much at stake. Follow the sparrow to the Mad King's castle."

It was strange how calm and focused she seemed, even though her words were crazy. "Sure, Mom," Atticus said soothingly. His gaze darted toward the door. He wished his father would get back. "The Mad King's castle. Got it."

"Darling boy . . ." Suddenly, her gaze unfocused and she tightened her grip as the pain came.

"Nurse!" Atticus shouted.

"Promise me," she whispered.

"I promise, Mom."

"My papers. Look in my papers. Promise."

"I promise."

"Grace," she whispered. "I need grace."

His mother had never been religious. "Do you want me to get the chaplain?"

She shook her head, frustration and pain on her face. "Vespers," she whispered through cracked lips. "The oldest of enemies. Guardian, promise me."

"I promise," he said, for the last time.

One last, gasped sentence. "Stay friends with Dan Cahill."

She closed her eyes, and her hand went limp. She died two hours later.

Now the agony of that night swept over him again, and he wanted to crash to his knees and sob. He wasn't over his mother's death.

But he had to be strong. He had to figure this out. Deathbed promises, made in a swirl of words he didn't understand. The pain in her eyes. The way she gasped for breath.

What if those things she was trying to tell him . . . were real?

Stay friends with Dan Cahill. He'd thought she was just reassuring herself that her son would continue his only friendship after her death. But now, in his head, he heard her voice. He heard the *urgency* of it.

He glanced desperately at his brother. How could he find the words to tell him? Jake would never believe him about Astrid. He'd say she was delusional, that she was full of painkillers. . . .

Jake was already dialing.

"Please, Jake!"

The desperate emotion in his voice made Jake stop.

Atticus thought fast. He had to give Jake a reason to go find Amy and Dan. His brain was suddenly firing with connections, and he had a feeling that only Dan and Amy could answer his questions.

"Interpol won't listen," he said. "Maybe you're right — what if Dan and Amy are after something else? And they're using Dad's name. What if they implicate him in the crime?"

"All the more reason to call the authorities," Jake said.

"No," Atticus said. "All the more reason to go to Prague."

CHAPTER 19

Kutná Hora was a picturesque city that had once sat on top of Europe's most prosperous silver mine. Back in medieval times, it was second only to Prague in importance. St. Barbara's Cathedral was renowned for its Gothic magnificence, and the town was popular with tourists. Amy and Dan milled with them as they exited the train station. Most headed for the cathedral or the mining museum in a fifteenth-century castle.

"Do you know what the Czechs used to do with people they didn't like back in ye olde medieval days?" Dan asked Amy. "Throw them out the window. Really, I read it on the train. It's called *defenestration.* It happened in the fourteen hundreds. And there was this event called the Great Defenestration in the sixteen hundreds, where this one group of guys threw this other group of guys they didn't like out the window of Prague Castle. They actually lived, because they landed in a dung heap. Now, there's a soft landing. But it started a trend. There's actually an *index entry* for defenestrations in the guidebook. Isn't that crazy?"

"Since when are you interested in history?"

"I'm not. I'm interested in wild acts of defenestration. Do you think we could arrange to meet Casper Wyoming in Prague Castle?"

"Sure. Keep thinking, Dan. Come on, let's find the bus."

Amy bought bus tickets at a *tabac* and asked directions to the bus for Sedlec. It was an easy walk to Masarykova Street.

The ride to Sedlec wasn't long, and soon they were pulling up in a small suburb. They jumped off the bus with several other passengers. A tourist with a camera and a backpack approached them. "Is this the way to the bone church?" he asked Amy.

"You mean All Saints?" Amy asked. "I think it must be that church up ahead."

"The *bone* church?" Dan murmured as he walked away.

Tucked next to the side of the church was a cemetery. Dan saw a skull and bones, like a Jolly Roger, at the entrance.

A real skull. With real bones.

"Cool," he breathed. "It's like the Church of Pirates."

They paid their money and walked in. There were a few others in the chapel, walking back and forth, studying the decorative garlands, the splendid white chandelier, and the sculptures against the walls.

It was all fairly magnificent — and then you noticed what everything was made of.

"It's all bones," Dan said in awe. "Human bones! Is this the coolest thing in the world, or the creepiest? Or both?" He glanced over at a skull sitting on a pile of finger bones. "Dude? Can you lend me a hand?"

The skull stared back, its lower jaw missing. "Cat got your tongue?" Dan asked.

Amy grinned. She was always glad to see the goofball in Dan reappear. She consulted the pamphlet. "There are the bones of at least forty thousand people here. Lots of them died of the plague. When they built the church above us, they turned this chapel into an ossuary—a place for bones. But there were so many that in 1870 they finally asked this guy to . . . uh, arrange them. So he did this."

"What a cool ye olde spookmaster dude," Dan approved.

They walked around in awe. What Amy had thought were carved stone garlands hanging from the balconies above were arm and leg bones. A skull stared at them blankly, a leg bone clamped between its jaws.

"The chandelier is made up of every human bone," Amy whispered to Dan as they looked above their heads.

Despite the creep factor, there was something so beautiful about this place, Amy thought. The fluttery edges of the hip bones looked like enormous flowers. The lineup of finger bones was a delicate necklace. A carved, painted cherub blew into a golden horn while casually balancing half a skull on its knee.

Dan wandered over to an alcove. Behind a wire screen was a mound of bones stacked in perfect rows. Alternating rows of skulls sat on the arranged bones. Their hollow eyes stared out. Some almost seemed to have expressions. One leaned over, resting on the next one, and Amy found herself drawn into those black, black eyes.

Somehow the creepy feeling left her. Death surrounded her, but here she and Dan were standing, living and breathing, and all these bones were just evidence of many lives lived before hers.

Dan gripped the wire grating. He moved closer to the skulls, staring, staring. His lighthearted mood was suddenly gone. Amy felt a flutter of alarm. What was he seeing?

"We're breathing in death," he murmured. "Every day." He half turned to Amy. "Everybody dies. Why do we run away so hard and so fast, when it's always there?"

"We run away hard and fast because *we don't want to die*," Amy said.

Dan seemed mesmerized by the black holes in the skull. Amy was afraid of his expression.

Dan shook his head. "It all seems so . . . futile."

"Futile?" Amy had never heard Dan use that word before. "You mean, pointless?"

"Yeah. I know the meaning of the word, Amy. I'm not quite as dumb as everybody thinks I am. I know, I've got the photographic memory, but you've got the brains, right?"

Dan's tone was sarcastic. Not teasing, but flat and almost mean.

"Not right," Amy said, shocked. Was that what Dan really thought? "Nobody thinks that."

Dan turned his back on her to gaze at the bones. "Futile. Stupid and pointless."

Amy took a breath. She felt the hurtful sting of Dan's tone, but she had no urge to stamp off. There was something heading for Dan, something that cast a huge shadow, and her first instinct was to grab his arm and pull him away from the darkness she saw. But that would just make the darkness grow.

"It doesn't seem that way to me," she said. She kept her voice quiet. "It seems to me that we're doing what all these people did. Just . . . trying to live in the best way we can. Protecting the people we love. We give it everything we have. Just like these people probably did."

Dan didn't say anything. It was like he hadn't even heard her.

"And I don't think you're stupid," she added fiercely.

She felt her cell phone buzz in her pocket. She checked the ID. Sinead.

"Are you in?" Sinead asked.

"We're in. Nothing to see. Nothing but old bones."

"Listen, I have another lead. We're certain now that the text that Cheyenne got was not from a mobile device."

"Meaning it was from a computer? In the church?"

"Exactly. And we figured out the *altitude* of the computer. It's about six feet down from where you're standing."

Amy looked around. The church and chapel were up a slight rise and looked down on the cemetery. She walked a few feet away so that no one could overhear.

"So there must be a room below us," she whispered.

"Exactly. Look around. And keep the line open, okay?"

"Okay, we're moving." Amy slipped on her earpiece and motioned to Dan. She saw with relief that he seemed to have shaken off his mood.

They walked around the perimeter of the church, under the fantastic ropes of bones. They cruised down the opposite side. A door had a sign in Czech, and they hesitated.

"It could say *welcome*, or it could say *keep out*," Amy said.

"Maybe we should do a spell-Czech," Dan said, opening the door.

The door led to a narrow flight of stairs made of large pieces of stone. They were worn in the middle from the thousands of feet that had traveled down and up over the centuries. Dan closed the door behind them, and immediately they were plunged into darkness. Amy got out her penlight and shined it on the stairs. They crept down. The place smelled ancient and damp. The roof was low above their heads. It dripped.

When they reached the bottom, she swung the

penlight along a narrow passageway. Even here, bones hung in garlands and were arranged in displays. Skulls lined a shelf that ran the length of the passage.

"I can't see anything on the video feed," Sinead said. "What is it?"

"It must be the passage to the cemetery," Amy said. "I can't imagine keeping a computer down here."

"Amy? Look at this." Dan stood in front of a metal grate. Behind it was a small room. He pushed open the grate and walked in. It was like a mini-amphitheater, only with dead people as patrons. Skulls were arranged in piles around the room, stacked atop leg bones and hip bones. Flat, narrow ledges ran around the room, serving as seats. There was a clear, flat, raised space along the far wall. Over it was an arrangement of bones in the shape of a giant letter.

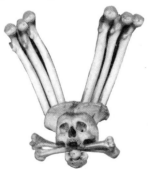

"Maybe the original guy who did the chapel — maybe he was a Vesper," Amy whispered. Somehow, whispers seemed appropriate here.

Dan moved around the space. "Look at this candle." He held out a candle with wax dripped down into the holder. "It's been used recently—there's no grime or dust in the wax."

"But there's no computer here," Amy said. "Please don't tell me we have to dig through the bones."

"No, look how they're arranged—it would be impossible to move them and stack them again so perfectly. I think you're right—it must have been a laptop."

"But there had to be a power source," Sinead insisted in Amy's ear. "Can you find an outlet anywhere?"

Dan and Amy shined their penlights on the walls close to the floor. Suddenly, Dan caught sight of something. He knelt on the floor. "Whoa. This would be *so* easy to miss. Did they have USB ports in the Middle Ages?"

"Try it!" Sinead said quickly.

Dan fished in his pack for a cable and hooked up his computer to the USB port. He scanned the drive. Nothing came up. "It's been wiped."

"I'm going to hand the phone to Evan—he'll talk you through it. You might be able to scrape something off it."

Dan settled with his back against the wall, computer in his lap. As Evan read out a list of codes, he typed them into his computer. The USB icon flashed.

"I think something's coming through . . . it's a file." Dan clicked on it. "Some kind of report. But it's only a few sentences."

"Save it to your hard drive and then e-mail it here."

Dan read the document as he pressed SAVE. "It won't

save," he said. "Or send. It's encrypted somehow. And parts of it are blacked out."

V-1 report

infiltrated family w/two children. Left MA w/mission complete. Information successfully destroyed. No suspicion from G. Coverup successful. Mother deceased. Children are

"It's disappearing," Dan said. "The words are disappearing!"

"It's an automatic wipe!" Sinead cried. "There could be an alert attached to it. You'd better get out of there."

Dan flipped over onto his knees to quickly stuff the computer in his backpack. He held his penlight in his mouth. As he zipped the pack, the light wavered on the old stones. He stopped. Someone had carved their initials into the wall.

Amy stood at the door. "Come on, Dan!"

He ran his fingers over the carving.

"Let's go!"

Dan wrenched himself away.

As he followed Amy's wavering shadow down the passageway, it seemed to flicker and then fade. And the shadow behind him seemed to grow.

infiltrated family

two children

MA

information successfully destroyed

Mother deceased

no suspicion from G

And the initials seemed to flame and burn inside his brain.

A.J.T.

At the end of a passageway was another door, small with a pointed arch. There was only a sliding iron lock. Amy pushed it back and opened the door. Gray light flooded the passageway. They stepped out into a soft rain and picked their way through the graves.

"Amy," Dan said, stopping. The smell released by the rain was of dead leaves and cold stone, and he could taste it in his mouth. "Amy . . ."

His sister turned impatiently. "We have to make the bus. . . ."

"Amy." He spoke her name for the third time. Wasn't that the charm in every fable? Say a name three times? And the parent turns into a witch, a wolf, a beast.

"I saw initials carved there. . . . *A.J.T.* . . . and the report . . . it proves it."

"Proves what?

Dan wheeled to face her, anguish twisting his features. "That our father was a Vesper."

CHAPTER 20

Amy stumbled against the cold stone. She sat down and rested her forehead against the cemetery marker. It was like Dan was hurling stones instead of words.

"There were his initials, right there," Dan said. "And the date—he was eighteen. In some sort of weird, spooky Vesper hideout!"

"It's three letters in a certain combination," Amy said. "*A.J.T.* It could be Albert John Toboggan. It could be Adam Jeffrey Turquoise. It could be *anything*!"

"What about the document? Infiltrating a family in Massachusetts? Two children? Information *destroyed*? What information?"

Amy shook her head violently. "I don't believe any of this. You shouldn't, either. We've been through this before, Dan! We've already been afraid that our parents were the bad guys. We know they weren't!"

"And what about *no suspicion from G*? It's Grace!"

"There's a G in Jane's notebook, too."

"That could be Grace as well. What if Jane was a Vesper?"

"She wasn't a Vesper!" Amy barked this furiously. She had grown fond of Jane. She refused to believe she could have been part of such a despicable organization.

And her father couldn't have been, either.

"What if he's not dead?" Dan asked in a hushed tone. "What if he's *still* a Vesper?"

Amy shook her head as the enormous weight of Dan's words hit her. She swallowed, feeling sick. "No."

"The fire . . . he was concealing the evidence!"

"Isabel Kabra set that fire! We know that! And we buried him. They found his *body*, okay?" Amy was yelling now. "Don't you think Grace would have checked?"

"Checked what? Fingerprints? He died in a fire. Except maybe he didn't. *Somebody* did. How are we supposed to know who it was?"

"Dan, we were there that night. I remember parts of it. I *know* Dad was there. I *saw* him!"

"Yes, he was there. But maybe he escaped. Do you remember the circus girl? She said that V-One had a burn."

Amy stood back up on shaky legs. "This is all circumstantial. You're really jumping to conclusions."

"Are you the only one allowed to have instincts, Amy?"

"Our father was not a *Vesper*!" She glared at Dan with all the fury that blazed inside her. "Since when are you so quick to denounce him?" she demanded. "He was your hero!"

The lost look in Dan's eyes frightened her. "Since I grew up."

Even through her anger, Amy felt something pierce her heart. Fear. She was so afraid for her brother. Had he really lost his childhood? Was that what the Clue hunt had done?

The Vesper phone buzzed in her pocket. She felt revulsion rise in her throat. She hated Vesper One. She hated all of them. She accessed the text.

```
Greetings, children. Time is running out.
```

Amy scrolled down. It was a low-resolution photograph of the hostages. Clumped together, made to sit in a line in their jumpsuits. Staring at the camera.

CAM 2: WHO SHALL BE NEXT?

They returned to Prague in silence. Amy had sent a text to Attleboro, not trusting herself to speak.

NEED TO CONTACT ERASMUS IMMEDIATELY. HAVE HIM CALL OR TEXT US WITH A TIME TO SPEAK.

They sat in an outdoor café in Old Town Square, watching the darkness fall. Across the square, tourists gathered at the top of the hour to see the famous Astronomical Clock. Amy heard it bong six times. They ordered a dinner they didn't want. To Amy, it felt like the end of the world. They would get into the library somehow tomorrow; she had enough faith to know that. But whether they would find the de Virga or not . . .

A man moved along the buildings of the square, from shadow to shadow. He wore small, round blue-tinted glasses and had curly dark hair streaked with gray. In his black leather jacket and black jeans he looked like a shadow himself.

Erasmus slid into a chair opposite them and lifted one finger to hail the waitress. "I hear you need to talk to me." He spoke rapidly to the waitress in Czech.

"We didn't know you were in Prague," Amy said. "Sinead said you were on the way to Rome."

"I leave for Rome tonight."

He paused as the waitress put down a steaming cup of coffee. He took a sip. Behind the tinted glasses Amy knew his gaze was constantly roving, picking out possible danger, routes of escape. What Erasmus did before devoting himself to the Madrigals, she didn't know. But he had a Vesper database in his head, every scrap of information the Madrigals had been able to pick up over the centuries.

Amy was wondering how to ask the question when Dan just blurted it out.

"Was our father a Vesper?"

Erasmus took a careful sip of coffee. He leaned back and blew out a sigh as he stared out at the square. Then he took off his sunglasses. His eyes looked tired. He leaned forward again, his big hands cradling the cup. With every move and gesture Amy felt her heart sink. She wanted to run as far and as fast as she could to escape what was coming next.

"Yes," Erasmus said.

"The bro just *orders,*" Jonah said. "I'm not saying I don't like him. I'm just saying."

"I hear you," Hamilton said. He threw another T-shirt into his pack.

"It's my *plane,* bro. And he walks in, dressed so fine in his leather, and he says, 'We're going to Italy tonight,' and it's, like, say what?" Jonah zipped up his duffel. "I'd just like a vote. That's all."

Still talking, they rode down in the elevator and walked out into the lobby. A gray-haired woman in a gray jacket and a shapeless hat was just getting up from a chair. Just as they passed her, Hamilton slung his big pack over his shoulder and caught her on the side of the head. She stumbled, and her purse went flying.

"Oh, man, I'm so sorry." Hamilton and Jonah dropped their packs and quickly stooped over to help gather the items that had spilled.

"It is okay," the woman said in an Italian accent. She shook her wallet at Jonah playfully. "I know you. Jonah Wizard."

"Busted!"

"That is a funny choice of words. In American English, that can be slang for . . . arrested, no?" The woman's brown eyes twinkled.

"Word. I should be careful, right?"

"You should be very careful." The woman flipped her wallet open. Inside they saw an ID card. Luna Amato was the woman's name. And then, in big black letters — INTERPOL. "Perhaps we can have a chat, no?"

Jonah and Hamilton exchanged glances. They had a feeling that answering "no" was not an option.

She directed them to a quiet corner of the lobby. She sat in an armchair, parking her purse on the floor. They sat on the edge of the sofa facing her.

"Just a little chat," she said in a friendly way. "You are here in Prague because . . . ?"

"Just chilling with my homey, doing the tourist thing," Jonah said.

"And your cousins, Amy and Dan Cahill? Are they enjoying the city as well?"

Jonah's heart sank into his running shoes. "Whoa, are they here, too? You know, I've got a bunch of cousins. Can't keep track of everybody."

"It seems to me," Luna Amato said, "it would be easy to keep track of people who travel with you on your private plane."

"What do you want?" Hamilton asked.

"Ah, let's cut to the chase, as they say in American movies, no?" Luna Amato leaned forward. "I am hoping you will take a message to Amy and Dan Cahill. We know they have *Il Milione.*"

Jonah kept his face expressionless. Hamilton stiffened.

"*Che macello!* What a mess! The lost manuscript! And these two children steal it! Why? To sell it? But they have a fortune already. To keep it? But they are not known as art lovers. I have seen children manipulated and forced to do things they do not want to do. I say to myself, maybe this is the case with these two."

"So what is the message?" Jonah asked.

Luna Amato sighed. "My partner, Milos Vanek—we are not alike. To him, if you steal something, you are a criminal. He does not believe in mercy. He believes in law. He will not listen to what they say. I will listen. Perhaps even I can help." Her face was intent. "Do you understand? They will need a friend at Interpol. I am that friend."

She gave them her card. Then she picked up the purse and walked out without looking back.

"Dude," Hamilton said.

"Dawg," Jonah said. "I can't tell if I'm scared of her, or I want her to bake me cookies."

CHAPTER 21

The lights glowed around the square. The rain had cleared and freshened the air. But the evening was chilly, and most of the patrons now sat inside in the warm, lit café. Dan and Amy sat outside at the table, their dinners cold and untouched. Amy found she was hugging herself tightly, her fingers digging into her arms.

"He was recruited," Erasmus said. "As Vespers often are, when they're young. Arthur was in college. When he told Grace the story, he made it clear that he had no idea that the Vespers were a criminal organization. He was fascinated by the fact that, at that time, scientists and engineers and historians were part of the group. There were hints of famous scholars in history being Vespers, people Arthur admired. He was approached by Vesper One—the former Vesper One. We know that he died about three years ago."

"But that means he knew who Vesper One was," Dan said.

Erasmus shook his head. "He never knew. There's

a courting period where they indoctrinate you—you don't know anyone's real identity at first. There's an initiation ceremony. Arthur was attracted to certain parts of the Vesper heritage, I admit. He was young, ambitious, maybe too impulsive for his own good. But after . . . uh, certain details of the Vesper philosophy came to light, he was horrified. He renounced the Vespers and married your mother. Your father is one of the reasons we know as much as we do about the Vespers."

"What about the Sedlec Ossuary?" Dan asked. "Why didn't he tell you about that?"

The challenge in Dan's voice made Erasmus frown.

"I'm guessing that was the site of his initiation," Erasmus said. "He was blindfolded and taken there. He only knew it was somewhere near Prague."

"So he never . . ." Amy swallowed. "He never did anything bad."

Erasmus turned his gaze to Amy. "I knew your father. He was a good man."

"Thank you for telling us," Amy said.

"You can count on me anytime," Erasmus said. He slipped his sunglasses into his pocket. "Remember this: We're on a dangerous path. But we have been on it for centuries. We will prevail."

As silently and gracefully as he had appeared, he left. Within moments, Amy could not tell where he'd gone. She could see only shadows where he had been.

Amy woke up to a gray morning. She didn't know if she'd really slept. The dreams were so real . . . the blurred memory of her father swinging her into a grocery cart, stringing pink fairy lights all over her bedroom to surprise her for a birthday, making a suit out of bubble wrap and declaring himself King Bub the Invincible.

Could that man be a Vesper?

She'd tried to talk to Dan about it, but Dan had withdrawn into himself. The muscles of his face pulled tight, and his eyes went flat. She wanted to shake him, as though she could shake good memories into him, the things about their father that he couldn't remember.

But then she remembered other things. Coming into the room and just catching the end of an argument between her mother and her father.

"What aren't you telling me, Arthur?"

The look on his face when he didn't know she was watching him. Staring into the fire in the study, gripping the book at his side, the orange flames flickering on the taut line of his mouth . . .

Dan looked so much like him.

So he never . . . he never did anything bad.

I knew your father. He was a good man.

Amy realized something: Erasmus had not really answered her question. Could good men do bad things? A question asked by a good girl . . . who had stolen, lied.

Amy threw back the covers. She hurried into the bathroom to wash her face and brush her teeth. She dressed quickly, pulling on her jeans and the same T-shirt she'd worn the day before. She smoothed out the wrinkles as best she could. Sooner or later, they'd have to find a Laundromat.

By the time she came out of the bathroom, Dan was awake and staring out at the city. He walked past her without saying good morning. She knew he wasn't angry at her. She knew he was thinking.

She just didn't know what he was thinking about.

She checked her e-mail accounts. A short e-mail from Ian.

Found UK professor (Lucian branch) willing to send evidence of your scholarly credentials to library. Stay tuned.

That was good news. Considering the time difference, she might have heard something already. She checked the separate, secure account and saw the e-mail. Holding her breath, she clicked on it.

Dear Miss Teague,
Your authorization to study at the library came through. You may come this morning at 10.
Katja Mavel

Amy felt relief flow through her. Not just because they'd gained access to the library. But because she wouldn't have to think about her father anymore.

"Dan! Hurry up! We're in!"

They hurried through the steel doors of the library. In the vestibule, along with the single polished-steel umbrella stand, two boys were waiting.

Amy and Dan stopped short. It was Atticus and Jake Rosenbloom. Atticus wore a hat with earflaps. Jake wore a scowl. Dan stood on one foot, poised to run.

Amy remembered the last time she'd seen Jake. She'd just kicked him in the ribs, hard enough to take his breath away. She remembered his look of surprise and outrage as he fell over backward onto the hard stones of the Colosseum. That had been one satisfying kick.

"Wait!" Atticus said excitedly. "We just want to talk to you! Please!"

The pleading in his voice made Dan pause. "What are you doing here?" he asked.

"Don't try to stop us," Amy said, looking at Jake. But it was an empty threat, and she knew it. She glanced around, looking for the Interpol agents.

"We came alone," Atticus quickly said. "This isn't a trap."

"Why should we believe you?" Amy countered.

Her gaze flicked to Jake. "You turned us in."

"Of course we did!" Jake exclaimed. "You stole a priceless historical document!"

"And you went running right to security, didn't you?" Amy said scornfully.

"You bet I did. Because it was the right thing to do!"

"Are you going to do it again, right now?" Amy asked furiously. "Or would you like another kick in the ribs?"

She adjusted her pack as though ready to strike. She *wanted* to. He deserved it.

"Look, the only reason I'm here is to protect my father. You're using his name to get something. Steal something." Suddenly, Jake reached out and grabbed her pack. "Is it in here?"

She went after him, grabbing at the pack. "Hey!"

Jake already had it open. Amy's crumpled T-shirts fell out, along with her research materials. One sheet of paper drifted down and landed at Atticus's feet.

The face of Jane Sperling at nineteen stared up at them. The photo had been pulled off the Internet, and it was grainy and dark. Laughing eyes, black hair to her shoulders, dressed in a belted gray coat, standing by a bare tree. The wind must have been blowing, because a filmy scarf almost obliterated her smile.

Atticus picked up the paper. He stared down at it, then up at them. "What are you doing with a picture of my great-grandmother?"

CHAPTER 22

Nobody spoke as they walked down a narrow alley that opened into a small, empty square. Atticus clutched the picture against his chest.

"Why do you have this?" he asked again.

Instead of answering, Amy posed a question. "What do you know about your great-grandmother?"

"Not much," Atticus said. "She lived in Maine. She was Jewish, but she married an African American soldier, back when you just didn't do stuff like that."

"Why do you have the photo?" Jake demanded. "We should be the ones asking questions, not you."

"Before the war, Jane Sperling was a student in Germany," Amy said.

Atticus nodded. "She was a medieval scholar."

"She spent the war years in London. She was an American spy."

Jake let out a surprised bark of a laugh. "Now I know you're crazy. A spy?"

But Atticus looked interested. Amy saw the flash of curiosity in his eyes. "Why do you think that?"

"Never mind why. Her code name was Sparrow."

"Sparrow!" Atticus gave a start. He looked down at the picture again. "Follow the sparrow to the Mad King . . ." he murmured.

"The Mad King?" Amy asked insistently. "Why did you say that?"

"It's something my mother said . . . the night she died. She was trying to tell me something. She'd been unconscious for days, and then she came to and talked to me."

"You never told us that." Jake looked at his brother in surprise.

"She said that I had to follow the sparrow to the Mad King's castle. I mean, what would you think?"

"I'd think she was delirious."

Amy gripped the notebook deep in her pocket. "Did she say anything else?"

"Oh, crazy stuff," Atticus said. "She kept talking about vespers and grace. She said she needed grace. Which is funny, because she wasn't religious at all."

"Grace?" Amy questioned sharply. "What if it was the *name* Grace? Like she was talking about a person?"

"She didn't know anyone named Grace," Jake broke in. "Atticus, why didn't you tell me this, or tell Dad?"

"Because it didn't make sense. And because . . ." Atticus hesitated. "Because I couldn't talk about it somehow. It was like a dream. She talked about this story she told me when I was really little. A bedtime story. I can barely remember it. There was this brave family in it who protected a ring. . . . I don't remember the name. Something to do with music. Or a poem."

"Madrigal," Amy said.

"Yes! That's it! There was a ring, and the Madrigals had to protect it. There was a dragon named . . ." Atticus looked up as knowledge lit his face. "Vesper! The dragon was named Vesper. That's all I can remember. She just kept saying 'the ring, the ring.'"

Amy had to stop herself from touching her watch. She had trained herself not to keep checking it was there. The ring wasn't a fantasy story. It was real, and resting against her skin.

"Would somebody please explain to me what's going on?" Jake cried in frustration. "Because I feel like I'm in some sort of cracked fairy tale."

Amy took out the notebook. "We found this in Neuschwanstein Castle, hidden in a drain. It belonged to Jane Sperling." She handed the book to Atticus.

"In the castle? So maybe I was meant to find it!" He opened the flap reverently.

To G: dV528.112K
Stolen by Hummel
repatriated w V. Kepler
resting w/ teacher & victim
together with the spellbound wanderer will point the way

Atticus looked up at them. "What does it mean?"

"We think 'dV' refers to the de Virga world map,"

Amy said. "We know for sure that Jane was interested in it."

Jake frowned. "I don't know what that is."

"It's a medieval world map that went missing in 1932. Your great-grandmother was at the auction when it was stolen." Amy quickly related their theory about what happened to the map. "Hummel stole it, and Jane got it back. Then she led us here."

"I see!" Atticus exclaimed. "So the numbers are a library collection number. And of course 'spellbound wanderer' is a no-brainer."

"Maybe to you," Dan said. "I'm clueless."

"Marco Polo," Atticus explained. "It's a quote from *Il Milione*. It's how Marco Polo refers to himself."

Amy groaned. "We should have guessed that!"

"But why do *you* want the map?" Jake asked. His eyebrows came down and he squinted at Amy suspiciously. She felt a flare of annoyance.

Atticus jumped in before she could answer. "But what's this about teacher and victim?"

"We don't know," Dan said. "Something that happened in the war, maybe?"

"Not the war," Jake said slowly, still looking at the notebook. "Hundred of years before that. Kepler worked for Tycho Brahe, the Danish astronomer. Brahe worked and died in Prague. There are theories that he was poisoned. His body was even exhumed recently—he died of mercury poisoning. Some people say that Kepler did it. So is there a Kepler manuscript here?"

Dan nodded. "We think Jane left a lead with it—or, we're hoping, the map itself."

"But why?" Jake asked, dark eyes on Amy's. It was annoying that he kept asking the right questions.

He was still suspicious, but he was curious now. He was learning things about his extended family he'd never dreamed of. Welcome to the club.

"Maybe we'll find out today," Amy said. "If we find the map."

"Okay, this all makes a weird kind of sense," Jake said. "If you're a totally illogical kind of person." He looked at Amy when he said it.

"Or it doesn't make any sense if you're a total resistant blockhead," Amy shot back.

He glowered at her. "You still aren't answering my question. What does this have to do with you two?"

"We can't tell you that," Amy said. "It's not just our secret. But we can tell you that lives are at stake. You just have to trust us." She raised her chin and looked him in the eye. "You know, sometimes the right thing isn't the thing you *think* is right. It's the wrong thing you're afraid to think of."

"When I figure out what that means, I'll let you know."

"Don't you want to know if Atticus's great-grandmother was a spy who had her hands on a medieval mappa mundi?" Amy asked.

"C'mon, Jake," Atticus urged. "We have to get inside!"

She saw in a flash that despite all Jake's doubts, he

couldn't walk away. His curiosity would lead him forward. Without another word, she turned and headed toward the library. She knew he'd follow.

In just a few moments, she heard footsteps and his voice behind her. "Just don't steal it," he said.

Amy decided it was better not to answer.

With the sons of Mark Rosenbloom with them, Amy and Dan had no problem getting into the library. They were ushered into the restricted section. Katja Mavel personally led them to the Renaissance collection. It was kept in a humidity-controlled room.

"You will have to leave your backpacks out here," she said, pointing to a rack outside the room. "No packs, purses, pens, or pencils are allowed. There is a computer inside for your use in taking notes. You may send the notes to the printer."

Dan, Amy, and Atticus put their backpacks on the rack. They walked into the collection room. The door shut behind them with a sharp click.

"This looks state-of-the-art," Jake remarked.

"Absolutely," the librarian replied. "Temperature and humidity controlled, halon gas fire protection system, all documents stored in archival boxes that are kept in fire-resistant metals. Oh, you know the halon system? It depletes the oxygen in the air in case of fire, to protect the materials. So if the alarm goes off, you must exit immediately. The door will automatically lock within two minutes. And of course you must wear the gloves if you touch the materials."

"Of course," Dan said. He pulled on a pair of white cotton gloves and splayed his fingers. "And they're also so helpful for jazz hands."

Katja Mavel opened a case and withdrew a long, flat box with the call letters Jane had jotted in the notebook. It looked faded and a bit battered. "Ah, this is one of the old boxes. Not much call for these materials. We are updating all the boxes, but it takes time." She put down the box but lingered. "So. You are studying the works of Tycho Brahe and Kepler?"

"Such a fascinating story," Amy said.

"Yes, you know, Brahe is quite a hero in Prague. His death . . . for so many years, scholars thought his bladder burst."

"Excuse me?" Amy asked.

"You know, he was at this great banquet, and it was said he didn't want to be rude and get up for the bathroom, so . . ."

Amy could feel Dan and Atticus trying not to giggle.

"We have a saying when we leave the table for the bathroom. We say 'I don't want to pull a Brahe.'"

Dan coughed. It was a strangled sound, as if he was smothering a laugh. Amy felt laughter bubble up inside her just at the sight of Dan's red face. This always surprised Amy, how hilarity could suddenly sweep over them just when things were at their most tense.

"So what exactly are you studying about Brahe?"

Katja Mavel asked.

Amy knew the question wasn't a trap. But they had to get rid of Mavel if they were going to steal the map.

Jake cleared his throat. "You know, my father still remembers his visit here so fondly," he said.

Katja Mavel blushed. "I remember him fondly as well—as a colleague." She tucked a dark strand behind her ear. "I admire his work. His scholarship. We all do. Is your father working on another book?"

Jake smiled. "I'd love to tell you a bit about it. I had a long train ride from Rome. I was wondering if there was any tea or coffee available . . . ?"

"Yes, of course. Why don't you come to my office. . . . Would anyone else care for refreshments?"

"No, thank you," Atticus said.

Jake took the woman's arm. "My father would be glad to know that the library is still doing such important work." As they walked away he looked over his shoulder at them. The look plainly said *work fast*.

Amy felt a twinge of annoyance. Jake could sure work the charm when he had to. He must know how gorgeous he was. And that made him insufferable.

"Ready?" Atticus asked them. His hands hovered over the box.

Biting her lip, Amy nodded.

Atticus lifted the lid. A musty smell invaded the room. Inside was the leather-bound edition of *Mysterium Cosmographicum*.

With the reverence of a scholar, he carefully turned

the pages. "It's in Latin," he said. "My Latin is pretty good, but I can't translate the entire book."

"I don't think Jane wanted us to," Amy said. "She hid the map somewhere inside the pages. I'm sure of it."

"Just shake the book," Dan advised. "Something will fall out."

Atticus looked horrified. "Shake a sixteenth-century book? I couldn't do that."

"I could."

Atticus emitted a squeak as Dan grabbed the book and turned it upside down. Nothing fell out. Atticus snatched the book back and hugged it.

"Dude, it's a book, not a puppy," Dan said.

"Let's examine the endpapers," Amy said.

Carefully, Atticus opened the book again. "Nothing in the front." He turned the book over. "Wait a second . . . there's something here. It's like the book has been repaired. I mean, that makes sense . . . it's more than four hundred years old. . . ." He peeled back a small section of endpaper. "There's something under here," he said excitedly. "I think we found the map!"

Cheyenne peeked over her book. Amy and Dan had disappeared into one of the side rooms with that skinny kid. The hunky teenager had gone into the library director's office.

Casper lurked in the stacks. Cheyenne closed her

book and joined him.

"The map has got to be here," Cheyenne said. "We can trail them after they leave. There are some dark alleys between here and their hotel. I know you're looking forward to that."

"I have a better idea, and it's even more fun," Casper said. "We can get rid of them in one stroke *and* steal the map."

"In one stroke?" Cheyenne asked doubtfully.

"One stroke of a match." Casper waved at the books in the stacks. "This will go up like a torch. But I can set the fire so that it doesn't burn down the whole place—though, let's face it, who would miss a *library*?"

Cheyenne nodded. "Totally."

"Here's the best part—I checked out the fire system in the research rooms with the old stuff—halon! Sucks all the oxygen out of the room. Turns you into a fish on a dock." Casper grabbed his throat and made gasping noises. "The whole place shuts down while we evacuate, I make sure the Cahills get stuck in the room of no air, they turn the systems back on, and we sneak back in and grab the map while the dead bodies of Amy and Dan look on. Presto change-o, we are winners!"

Cheyenne waved at the stacks. "You would destroy thousands of priceless antique books and papers just to get your hands on that map?"

"Is that so wrong?"

"Cool," Cheyenne said. "I'm in."

CHAPTER 23

Atticus peeled back the last of the endpaper. A parcel was folded flat and wrapped in paper. A piece of note-paper sat on top.

"It matches the paper from Jane's notebook," Amy murmured.

Atticus read it aloud in a nervous voice.

V Kepler killed his teacher, G Brahe, for this, but could not decipher what he needed to know. The map needs a partner.

The murderer points to the genius, who hides the traveler. And the wind rose on the traveler's road and pushed him toward the city of stars. G, if you need to move it, hide it well. JS

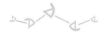

"There's that G again," Amy murmured. "Grace?"

"No," Atticus whispered. "Guardian." He seemed

to be in a daze, staring down at Jane's note.

Before Amy could ask him what he meant, Dan broke in impatiently.

"C'mon. Let's see what the parcel is."

"Right." Atticus unfolded the parcel and spread it on the desk. Amy recognized it immediately.

"It's the de Virga!" she exclaimed. "Thank you, Jane!"

"It's amazing," Atticus breathed.

It just looked like an old map to Dan, but he leaned over to study it. "What's that?" he asked, pointing to a spot.

"That's the compass rose," Atticus murmured. "Shows the direction of the compass. It's right over Central Asia. The detail on this thing is amazing. Look at the coast of Africa!"

A light began blinking red over their heads. Amy

looked up just as the siren went off. "Great. What a time for a fire drill."

"We've got to conceal the map somehow," Dan said.

"Wait a second," Atticus said. "You guys are going to *steal it*?"

"We have to," Amy told him.

"But Jake said—"

"Never mind Jake. Dan, can you get it under your sweatshirt?"

"Under his sweatshirt? Are you crazy?" Atticus cringed as Dan folded the parchment.

"Believe me, A, we've got a good reason," Dan told him.

"Atticus, can you go find Jake?" Amy asked. "We're right behind you. Whatever you do, keep Mavel away from here. And, um, there's no need to tell Jake that we stole the map. Yet."

Amy crossed to the window in the door. Library patrons packed up and were leaving in an orderly fashion. Suddenly, she spotted two tall blond young people. Casper and Cheyenne stood in a corner, watching. What were they doing here? Her pulse hammered out a frantic beat.

"Atticus, I need you to go now," Amy said, making sure her voice was level. "We'll explain everything outside. Tell Jake . . . tell him he has to trust me." Not that he would. But Amy couldn't put Atticus in danger.

Amy took a firm hold of Atticus's arm. She opened the door and gently shoved him out, then closed it.

To her shock, she heard the lock click. The automatic lock had engaged.

Atticus pulled frantically on the door. Amy tried to open it from her side. It wouldn't budge.

The halon gas!

She whipped her head around to spy the fire panel.

HALON GAS ACTIVATED

OXYGEN LEVEL 20%

This was no drill. This was really happening.

As she watched, the indicator beeped.

OXYGEN LEVEL 19%

Atticus took off at a run.

"Dan?" Amy's voice shook. "We have a problem."

"We sure do," Dan said, adjusting his shirt. "This parchment is really itchy."

OXYGEN LEVEL 18%

"I just saw Casper and Cheyenne outside. This isn't a drill! The halon gas suppression system has been activated! And the door is locked!"

Dan looked at the oxygen level, then made a run at the door. He pulled at it. Just then Casper Wyoming's face appeared at the glass panel. He waved and mouthed *"Bye-bye."*

Then he kept on walking.

"Atticus saw what happened," Amy said, her voice trembling. "He'll do something. . . . He'll get Jake!"

"With Casper and Cheyenne around? Don't count on it. We have to do something."

OXYGEN LEVEL 16%

Amy felt her pulse race. Was it the dropping oxygen level, or her own fear rising?

Dan began kicking at the door. Amy pounded on the glass.

There was nobody to hear. The building had been completely evacuated. Smoke was now billowing out of the stacks at the opposite end of the wide room. Amy saw orange licks of fire.

"We have to do something!" Amy's breath was short. The effort of pounding against the glass had exhausted her. That wasn't a good sign.

"The computer," she said to Dan. "It's hooked to the server. You could hack in—disrupt the alarm!"

Dan hurried over to the computer.

OXYGEN LEVEL 13%

"We have to hurry," Amy said. "Oxygen depletion affects your brain. You can't think. . . ."

"I'd have to get past the fire wall. . . ."

Amy felt her temples pound. "What was it that the hacker taught us? The back door option . . . you can get into their e-mail and go on from there. . . ."

"I remember, but I'm no Evan."

"You're just as smart as he is," Amy said firmly. "You can do it."

Dan began punching out a string of code.

OXYGEN LEVEL 11%

Looking over his shoulder, Amy tried to concentrate on Dan's numbers. It seemed like an incredible effort. Dan made a mistake and had to back up.

"I'm in!" Dan leaned forward. "Now to get Att . . . Attleboro. . . ." His breath was quick, and he wiped at the sweat on his forehead. "I've got Evan!"

Amy watched as Dan typed out HALON GAS CZECH LIBRARY SYSTEM HELP

It took a moment. Then they saw the words appear I'M ON IT

"He'll . . . have to . . . hack into the system through this terminal," Dan said.

Amy clutched the chair back as a wave of dizziness washed over her. "Dan . . ."

He looked over his shoulder at her. Perspiration streaked his face, and his eyes were glassy.

OXYGEN LEVEL 7%

They were close to passing out. Amy slid down to the floor. Dan slumped down next to her. She felt his hand reach for hers. If it was over, they'd go together.

Jake was out. Stretched on the ground, a lump on the back of his head and the world swimming in front of his eyes. One minute he was running after Atticus, the next, he was down. Some Nordic-looking guy had been next to him and suddenly managed—Jake wasn't sure how—to check him right into a wall.

He forced himself to his knees. He saw a screaming Atticus being held by a blond young woman. She appeared to be trying to hold him back from running back into the burning building. But she was gripping him too tightly. . . .

Atticus met his gaze. "DAN AND AMY!" he screamed.

The blonde pressed Atticus's head against her chest as if to comfort him. Jake saw with horror that she was actually muffling his scream.

He struggled to his feet. He had to get to his brother. But Dan and Amy were still in the library! Through the pounding pain in his head, he pushed forward, even before he knew which way to go.

Amy felt sick.

Dan's voice was weak. "He'll . . . do it. . . ."

She looked over at the oxygen indicator.

OXYGEN LEVEL 6%

The siren stopped. From somewhere far away she heard a click. The lock!

Fighting her nausea and weakness, Amy crawled to the door and reached up for the knob. It seemed so impossibly high. Her fingers grabbed at air. Finally, with an enormous effort, she raised herself up and gripped it. The door felt as heavy as iron. She yanked at it with all her strength, and it opened.

She fell forward into the hallway outside. She took a breath. It was smoky and it made her cough, but it was air. As oxygen filled her lungs, she felt stronger.

She made her way unsteadily back to Dan. He

was half conscious. She lifted him to his feet and half dragged him out the door.

He leaned over, coughing, taking shallow breaths.

They stumbled down the corridor. Two firemen appeared at the end of the hall. As soon as they saw Amy and Dan struggling to walk, they rushed forward.

Amy felt herself being lifted up and cradled like a baby. Coughing, she was carried out the door. The air felt so pure and sweet.

She saw Jake pushing through the crowd toward them, Atticus at his side. And, off to the side, the tall Wyoming twins walked rapidly toward the tram stop. Cheyenne was limping.

Amy felt too tired to care. She was laid down on a patch of cold stone and it felt as luxurious as a bed. An emergency technician checked her over and put an oxygen mask on her face.

"Is she going to be okay?" Jake asked. His concerned face swam in front of her.

"She'll be fine," the technician assured him.

Atticus hovered near Dan, almost in tears.

Dan lifted one hand slowly, patted his chest, and gave Amy a nod. He had the map.

CHAPTER 24

Rome, Italy

William McIntyre sat in his hotel room in Rome, file folders stacked to one side. He tried not to think about what time it was in Massachusetts. Jet lag lasted whole days for him now. His body felt tired, but he needed to push himself a little longer before he allowed himself to rest.

Amy and Dan were on his mind. He had the utmost confidence in their abilities, but that didn't mean he didn't worry constantly. He hadn't imagined anything could be more challenging and difficult than the search for the Clues, but this was proving to be so. Lives were at stake. And Vesper One . . . the fact that he could engineer this scheme, with hostages taken from all over the world . . . with kidnapping a boy of twelve . . . well, this was a new level of depravity.

He had confidence in all of them, not just Amy and Dan—Erasmus, Sinead, Ian, Hamilton, Jonah—

even that boyfriend of Amy's had turned out to be a worthy member of the team.

If only he didn't feel as though they were missing something.

Something crucial.

He had come to Rome to meet with Erasmus, but first, he needed to consult with a client. That little thing that was nagging at him—he needed to dig a little deeper. But the client meeting hadn't panned out. All he was able to get was a stack of old files.

McIntyre slipped the first folder off the stack and opened it. He began to read in his usual careful fashion. After plowing through a third of the stack, he suddenly straightened and began to read more intently.

He paused to kick off his shoes and order coffee and sandwiches from room service. He moved to the couch in order to spread out. He put some documents on the coffee table, separating them into piles.

It was with dawning horror that he realized that his instincts were right.

Why hadn't he seen these connections before? He had been such a fool.

Amy and Dan were in greater danger than he thought.

He jumped up to retrieve his secure cell phone to call Attleboro, but there was a knock at the door.

"Room service, *signore*."

Of course, the sandwiches. That was fast. He couldn't

imagine eating now, but he called, *"Entrare*—come in."

McIntyre kept his gaze on the paper he was reading. "Just put it on the desk, *per favore.*"

He stood to sign the bill. The waiter had his back to McIntyre as he put down the tray.

McIntyre had exactly three seconds to notice several things. Water glass not quite full. Napkin folded imprecisely. Smear of butter on the metal dome covering the plate.

He made the conclusion with equal speed. Someone had picked up a used tray from the hallway and then tried to make it look fresh.

He had only a few more seconds to react. With one glance at the waiter he knew he was in no shape to take him on. He would go down fighting, but the best he could do was leave something behind.

Behind his back, he crumpled the paper. Then he leaned down as if for his wallet and stuffed the paper in his empty shoe.

The waiter turned, and McIntyre saw his face for the first time.

For a long second, the two just stared at each other. Then the intruder rushed toward him.

"It's you!" McIntyre gasped.

The needle sank into his neck.

The smile on the face from the past was the last thing McIntyre saw before his knees gave way.

The firemen insisted that Amy and Dan get checked out at the hospital, but they refused. Katja Mavel either felt totally guilty or totally responsible and afraid to get sued, because she offered to take them to her own doctor. "But they were signed out!" she kept telling the firemen, wringing her hands.

In the end Amy prevailed, promising at the first sign of weakness or discomfort to head for a doctor. They were feeling fine, she told everyone earnestly. She was anxious to be gone. Her brother had a stolen map underneath his shirt.

"You should come with us," Atticus urged. "We're staying with this professor, a friend of our father's. The apartment goes on for miles—we even have our own sitting room. He won't mind if you stay, I guarantee it."

Amy glanced at Jake. "Sure," he said flatly. "You can fill us in on why somebody's trying to kill you. And who those blond thugs were, and why they targeted me and Atticus."

"I saw them leaving," Amy said. "The girl was limping."

"She needed a little persuasion to let my brother go," Jake said. "Any idea why they were there?"

Amy didn't say anything. She knew they'd have to spill some details, but she wasn't sure how much to tell. They needed the help of the Rosenblooms right now. Soon, Vesper One would demand the transfer. Before they gave up the map, they had to figure out its connection to *Il Milione*.

As they trudged to the apartment, Amy dropped back, letting the three boys walk together. She took a moment to text back to Attleboro. She needed advice. Who better than Sinead? She totally trusted Sinead's coolheaded opinion on things.

WE ARE FINE. HAVE MAP. JAKE AND ATTICUS HERE IN PRAGUE. THEY DEMAND ANSWERS. THEY GOT US INTO LIBRARY AND CAN BE HELPFUL W MAP AND MILIONE. THINK WE NEED TO CONFIDE SOME DETAILS ABOUT VESPERS, HOSTAGES, ETC.

ASK ERASMUS AND MCINTYRE ABOUT GUARDIANS.

In a few minutes, Sinead texted back:

NO INFORMATION ON GUARDIANS FM ERASMUS. MCINTYRE NOT ANSWERING. BEWARE. ROSENBLOOM BROTHERS TURNED YOU IN ONCE. WOULD DO IT AGAIN. STRONGLY ADVISE NO.

Amy slipped the phone back in her pocket, feeling strangely disappointed. She felt they owed Jake and Atticus more of an explanation. And she sensed that Atticus had more to tell them. But maybe Sinead was right. Certainly, Jake had turned them in once before. He could do it again. He could be lying to them right now. The two boys could be leading them straight to Interpol.

As Jake and Atticus reached a busy street corner, Jake put his hand on Atticus's shoulder for an instant. Atticus was so busy talking he would have blundered right into traffic. Amy studied that touch. It was brief, so that Atticus wouldn't feel directed by his big brother, but it was caring. She remembered the sight of Jake pushing through the crowd, trying to get to them, standing over her, making sure she was okay. He took responsibility for things, she could tell.

Just the way Jake felt responsible for *Il Milione*. Because, in a different world, under normal circumstances, Amy would have felt the same way.

Okay, she thought grudgingly, *I'll give him that. He cares.*

Maybe she shouldn't have kicked him *quite* so hard.

The apartment took up two floors of a grand building close to Old Town Square. Everything seemed to be upholstered in leather or velvet, and Amy had never seen so many tassels and trimmings—on curtains, on chairs, on sofas. Books were piled in short columns everywhere and used as tables for an assortment of abandoned teacups. At this hour, it was still and quiet.

Until Jake heard the news.

"You *stole the map*?" Jake asked furiously.

"We can explain—" Amy started.

"Do you realize that you've implicated my brother in your crime? And me?"

"I'm sorry, that was unavoidable. The fire alarm—"

"You said you were only going to *look* at it."

"No, actually, that's what *you* said," Amy corrected.

"She's right, Jake," Atticus said.

Jake wheeled on Atticus. "And you! How could you get involved in something like this?"

Atticus took a breath and faced his brother. "Because I'm a Guardian," he said. "I'm involved whether I like it or not."

"What's a Guardian?" Dan asked.

Jake held his head. "Not this wacko fairy-tale stuff again."

"It's not a fairy tale!" Atticus cried. "I know that now. Mom told me I was a Guardian. I didn't know what she meant. I still don't. But I think my great-grandmother was one, too." Atticus looked at them, vulnerable and scared. "Do you know what it means?"

"No. Can you tell us what she said?" Amy asked.

"I remember that she talked about the Guardians right before she got sick. She said it was a story her mother told her, only she never believed it. That there was this group that protected something over the centuries. More than one thing. They moved stuff from place to place until they found the safest spot. My mom thought it was a made-up story. But then she met someone who told her it was true. She didn't believe her, either. But this person said that the Guardians and the Madrigals were sort of partners. And that the Vespers were our enemies."

"Grace," Amy said. "That's why your mother called for her in the hospital. Grace is — was — our grandmother."

"Of course!" Atticus cried. "Because Mom suggested I join this online gaming group and look for this guy named Cahill. She said she'd met his grandmother once and thought we'd hit it off. And I thought you were really cool, so we became friends. Not because of her, but because . . ." Atticus's voice faltered as he added, "Because you liked me."

Dan held out his fist for a bump. "You are blowing my mind, dude."

Meanwhile, Jake stood a few paces away, his arms folded. Amy tried not to squirm. Whenever she felt his eyes on her, she grew annoyed. He couldn't just glance at a person. He had to *read* the person, as though he was waiting for her to make a mistake or pull something over on him.

"Listen, Miss Mysterioso, it's time we heard some answers. We're not going to go another step forward if you don't tell us what you're involved in. What exactly did you mean about lives being at stake? You and Dan almost suffocated. That wasn't accidental. Somebody is after you. Who is it? Who are the Vespers? What do they have to do with you?"

They were facing each other across the room, both of them with their arms crossed.

"I'm afraid to tell you," Amy said.

Jake's stern expression relaxed for a moment. "Did you ever think," he said slowly, "that we could help?"

Here it was—the moment Amy knew was coming. And she wasn't in the least bit prepared. Sinead had told her not to trust them. But Sinead wasn't in this room.

She remembered Jake's hand on Atticus's shoulder. She remembered him saying *Because it was the right thing to do.* She felt something odd insinuate itself inside her. She still didn't *like* him. But she trusted him. He was one of the good guys—she could feel it.

She looked at her brother. They had a moment of pure communication, the thing between them that they'd counted on during the hunt for the Clues. There were so many times that they trusted their instincts, ignored what they *should* do and proceeded to take a different way. It had worked out. Usually.

Yes, Dan's gaze was saying, *we can trust them. We have to.*

"Telling you what's going on could endanger you," Amy said hesitantly. "I know that sounds way dramatic, but it's true."

"We're already in up to our necks," Jake said.

Amy took a breath. There was so much to say, but she didn't have to say it all yet. "The Vespers are a group that's been in existence for hundreds of years—since the sixteenth century. It's a secret organziation, and its members are recruited. So we don't know any identities—well, we know two. The twins who were at the library. And your mother . . . She was right about the ring. They're after it. It's not magic, of course, but we don't know why they want it."

"Wait, hold on a second. Who's *we*?" Jake asked.

Amy and Dan didn't say anything. They couldn't just blurt out a secret that had been kept for hundreds of years.

But they didn't have to.

"You're Madrigals," Atticus guessed. "That story is true, too."

"Seven people from our family have been kidnapped," Dan said. "We almost were, too. And then we get this phone with a text on it from this dude called Vesper One. He says that if we don't follow his instructions, he'll kill them."

"Are you sure he's serious?" Jake asked.

"He shot one of them," Amy said. "In the shoulder. She seems okay, but . . ." She took a shaky breath to compose herself. "So yeah, he's serious."

Jake kept his gaze on Amy. "Are the people they kidnapped . . . are you close to them?"

Amy felt her eyes sting. She willed herself not to cry. She lifted her chin and tensed her whole body so it wouldn't happen. She couldn't appear weak in front of Jake. "We'll do anything to get them back."

She'd done everything to show him strength, but somehow, she sensed, he saw her vulnerability instead. He cleared his throat and looked out the window.

Dan got his computer out of his backpack and then

reached for *Il Milione*. "Okay, gang. It's time to get the jump on Vesper One."

" 'For to the world I was a Traveler, but once on the road I stopped in the great and splendid City. There I took on the task, Guardian, of what was entrusted to me to keep.

" 'Men steal and kill, they hide and conceal, and the great Task for us is to bury what should be buried and do not mourn, for it is better so.' "

Atticus read the words out loud. Then he pushed his glasses up on his forehead and rubbed his eyes. He'd found a dictionary of Old French in the professor's library, and it had taken him awhile to translate the epilogue.

"It's kind of rough," Atticus said. "My Old French isn't as good as my Latin."

"Are you sure the translation is correct?" Jake asked.

"Who are you talking to?" Atticus asked, insulted. "Of course it's correct."

" 'The great and splendid City' . . . there must have been a few on the Silk Road," Amy said.

"What's that?" Dan asked.

"It was an old trading route," Jake said. "It wasn't called the Silk Road back then."

"The term didn't come into use until maybe the late nineteenth century," Atticus put in. "I believe it was a German term at first?"

"Uh, smart dudes? This isn't *Jeopardy!*" Dan said.

"Can you just give me a summary?"

"Trading routes through Asia," Jake said, studying the de Virga map. "Look, the wind rose is right in Central Asia."

"I thought it was called the compass rose," Amy said.

"Same thing." Without touching the map, Jake passed his finger over the expanse of territory. "Four thousand miles or thereabouts, from the Mediterranean to China. That includes parts of Turkey, Uzbekistan, India, Persia, Afghanistan . . . that's a lot of territory. Maybe this will make sense if we look up some facts about cities along the route."

"Let's look at Jane's note again," Dan suggested.

V Kepler killed his teacher, G Brahe, for this, but could not decipher what he needed to know. The map needs a partner.

The murderer points to the genius, who hides the traveler. And the wind rose on the traveler's road and pushed him toward the city of stars. G, if you need to move it, hide it well. JS

"The murderer must be Kepler," Jake said. "And the genius?"

"Leonardo," Amy said. "His shield was concealing *Il Milione* at the Colosseum."

"The city of stars," Dan said. "What do you think

Jane meant? Could it be the great and splendid city that Marco Polo talks about? He's the traveler, right?"

Atticus was still consulting *Il Milione.* "Wait, there's a couple more sentences." He bent over the book again. In only a few minutes, he put down his pencil.

Remember this: For those pledged to Protection, long we have done this, for long shall we continue. To those who find this book, I pass to you the Duty I was given, as you shall pass to yours. The fate of the world is in our hands.

"That's extreme," Dan said. "The fate of the whole world? Exaggerate much?"

Amy noticed Atticus's look of distress. "What is it?" she asked.

"'The fate of the world is in our hands,'" Atticus said. "That's just what my mother told me. The night she died."

They all exchanged glances. This time, Dan stayed silent, and Jake didn't scoff. It seemed so crazy . . . *the fate of the world.* But suddenly, it seemed so real.

CHAPTER 25

Dan woke up with his face planted in a pile of papers. He had been dreaming about the wind. He pushed himself up, yawning and rubbing the indentations of balled-up paper on his cheek. The others had conked out, too—Jake in a deep armchair, and Atticus on the floor on a pile of quilts. Amy was asleep on the velvet sofa, her arms over her head, as if protecting herself.

The wind rattled the old panes of the windows and seemed to make the entire building creak with unease.

And the wind rose and pushed the traveler . . .

Dan suddenly felt wide-awake.

"Look, the wind rose is right in Central Asia."

"I thought it was called the compass rose."

"Same thing."

Jane had been talking about the wind rose on the map!

Dan's hands were shaking as he reached for the computer. He typed a word string into a search engine.

wind rose de Virga map

And the word popped up: *Samarkand*

He clicked on the link. It was a description of the de Virga map. It said that the wind rose was in Central Asia, "most likely over the city of Samarkand, where Ulugh Beg's observatory once stood."

Observatory? *The city of stars.* Jane had pointed them in the same direction!

It had been there all along, and it was all so much easier than he'd imagined! As though *Samarkand* was the magic word that unlocked every clue.

Dan did another quick word search. *The great and splendid city*—those were Marco Polo's own words, and they described Samarkand. Buried in the text of *Il Milione* . . . but readily popped up on a search engine. Dan's fingers flew on the keys. So this was why Amy got all excited when she researched! Piece after piece, falling into his hands, and they all made a picture.

Samarkand was the clue. And if they could get there first . . . maybe they could have a bargaining chip.

Dan crept over to where Amy lay sleeping. He put his hand on her arm and her eyelids sprang open.

"Samarkand," he whispered. "That's what he wants. If you put the map together with Marco Polo, that's what you get. The wind rose is right over the city."

"What?" Amy was wide-awake immediately. "Let me see."

He showed her his process, from putting together *wind rose* with the clues in Marco Polo's lost epilogue and Jane's hints.

"I think you're right," Amy whispered slowly. "This is such good work, Dan!"

Dan felt a glow at his sister's praise. He was known for his photographic memory. It was Amy who could take random information and form it into a theory. But tonight, he'd not only remembered things, he'd put them together.

Just then the Vesper smartphone buzzed by Amy's side. She accessed the message and turned the phone so that they both could read it.

```
Here's your alarm clock, and it's ticking!
Meet me at the Astronomical Clock at six
a.m. When the skeleton pulls the rope,
leave the packet at the feet of Jan Hus.
And don't look back!
```

"He's going to be there himself," Dan said. "He said 'meet me.'"

"It's twenty to six. We have to get moving."

"Where? What is he talking about, the skeleton pulling the rope? Who's Jan Hus?"

Amy put a finger to her lips. "Shhh. Don't wake Atticus and Jake." She grabbed for her shoes. "The Astronomical Clock is right in Old Town Square—it's one of the biggest tourist destinations in Prague. At the top of the hour, these mechanical carved figures come out in a procession—but first, a skeleton on the clock pulls a rope. The Jan Hus monument is there, too. We passed through part of the square on the way here, do you remember? It's about ten minutes away."

"That doesn't give us much time." Dan reached for his shoes.

Amy slipped the de Virga map into her pack. "Let's go."

Fog shrouded the dark city. It was still dark. The sun wouldn't rise until after seven A.M. No one was on the cobbled streets. Amy had mapped out the route and they slipped down the alley, made a right on an avenue, and continued toward the square, running as though a clock was ticking in their heads. Occasionally, they would see another figure in the fog, an early riser heading for work, someone walking a small dog.

As they approached the square their steps slowed. They had made it. Now the swirling fog enveloped them, magnifying every sound.

"Do you hear that?" Dan whispered. "Footsteps behind us."

Amy could hear them now, the quick steps of someone on the cobblestones.

They picked up their pace again. The monument to Jan Hus was a dark shape that they scooted past to run to the Town Hall, where the clock was located. It rose suddenly out of the gray mist. Amy checked the time on her watch. One minute to six.

There were other people on the square. It was large

and open, with restaurants and shops lining it, so there were people coming in to work. They could hear the footsteps and occasionally the sound of a murmured conversation. But the fog isolated them and kept them apart, staring up at the clock.

Was the fog lifting? The threads were twining around the clock tower. They could just make out the skeleton. A rope was in its hand. As they watched, the skeleton pulled the rope. The clock began to chime. Doors flicked open in the tower, and carved figures began to move jerkily forward.

"Now," Dan murmured.

They turned toward the monument. The fog gave them great cover. Dan jumped over the chain.

Amy quickly scanned the square. A white-paneled bakery truck was unloading trays of bread. A waiter whistled as he set out tables. An old woman sat at a table with a cup of coffee and a glass of ice. A mother walked by the tables, holding the hand of a small child. No one was looking at them.

Dan hoisted himself up over the base and placed the packet at the feet of Jan Hus.

"Dan! Amy!"

The voice seemed amplified through the fog. Amy started as she saw Atticus running at top speed across the square toward them.

Time seemed to slow down. And yet, everything happened so fast.

She heard the squeal of tires. When she looked up, she saw the bakery truck careening across the square. Atticus was still running toward them, on a collision course with the truck.

"ATTICUS!" she screamed.

The truck squealed to a halt.

Atticus bent over, hands on his knees, catching his breath.

Amy's hand was on her heart. She could feel the pounding, hard and fast. She had expected to see the truck hit the skinny body, send it flying.

The driver stayed at the wheel. The passenger got out and crossed to Atticus with quick steps, as though to ensure that he was all right. Then she recognized the figure in the long white apron.

It was Casper Wyoming.

"ATTICUS!" Amy screamed again.

She sprinted across the square, across the uneven paving stones. All her months of cross-country training paid off. She didn't stumble.

Atticus lifted his head, confused, as Casper grabbed his arm, twisted it back behind him, picked him up, and tossed him in the back of the truck.

"NO!" Amy screamed as she ran.

Dan suddenly appeared on her left. He had vaulted over the monument, making better time. In a last burst of speed, he threw himself at Casper.

Casper sent his elbow straight into Dan's throat.

Dan flew backward through the air, his head striking the paving stones with a thud that sent panic shooting through Amy.

The bakery van door slammed.

Sobbing, Amy reached Dan. She crashed to her knees.

"Dan!"

He was out cold. She pressed her cold fingers against his pulse. It skittered against her hand. "Dan!"

She looked up as the red taillights disappeared into the fog. "ATTICUS!" she screamed.

CHAPTER 26

Atticus could smell bread and motor oil, and it made him sick. The truck jounced over the uneven road, slowing down now, which didn't make the jolts any easier on his head.

When he'd seen movies about things like this, he'd always imagined how he'd react. Using his razor-sharp reflexes and boundless courage, he'd pull a surprise move and use a pencil to stab his abductor. Or he'd leap out of the way, jump onto the roof of a passing car, and escape.

Instead, he'd been picked up like a trussed chicken and tossed on a pile of bread. Before he could even cry out, a gag was stuck in his mouth, and then he'd been shoved in a sack with his hands tied behind his back.

And he was terrified. Maybe courage wasn't on his list of attributes after all.

He didn't want to be a Guardian. He didn't want to know the things his mother had told him. He didn't want any of this. He was a physical coward. Even Ferris wheels made him sick. He couldn't do this!

There was one chance. One tiny chance. If Jake would only think of it.

One tiny chance to find him.

Amy and Dan sat on a bench at the monument.

The de Virga was gone. So was *Il Milione*. It had been taken from Amy's backpack while she ran to save Atticus.

Amy tried to catch her breath. Her head whirled, and she felt dizzy and cold.

When her phone buzzed, she picked it up with dread in her heart.

Naughty, naughty. You had Il Milione all this time. You really shouldn't keep secrets from me. Your punishment this time: A Guardian goes down.

"That message that Hamilton saw on Cheyenne's phone," Amy said. "'*G is in the picture. Could need removal.*' Why didn't we realize that Atticus could be in danger! The message was about him!"

"We didn't know he was a Guardian then," Dan said. "And then things were happening so fast. . . ."

"The Vespers will kill him, Dan!" Amy held her head and rocked back and forth.

Just then they saw Jake stride into the square. He

scanned the space, and relief crossed his face when he saw them.

Amy and Dan stood up to face him as he came forward.

Tears ran down Amy's cheeks. "I'm so sorry," she said.

Rome, Italy

Erasmus stood in McIntyre's hotel room. He had dealt with the shock. The grief could wait. Grief would cloud his mind, and he needed to be clear.

McIntyre lay sprawled across the couch. A room service tray sat on the desk with the remains of a meal. Erasmus lifted the metal dome over the plate and sniffed. Shrimp. McIntyre was allergic to shrimp.

He pieced together the scenario. McIntyre had ordered room service and then the assailant had posed as a waiter. Picked up any random tray from the hallway, where people often put them instead of calling for pickup. Then after he was finished here, he'd called to cancel the order from the phone, so no one would come to the room until morning.

Erasmus checked the receiver. It had been wiped clean.

McIntyre had been working. His briefcase was open, and files were neatly stacked on the coffee table. Erasmus's gloved fingers flipped through them quickly. Client files, none of them seeming important. He filed the names away in his memory just in case.

McIntyre was dressed in pants and a shirt and tie, but in his stocking feet.

Things had been taken. Erasmus knew McIntyre was old-fashioned. He always traveled with a yellow legal pad. Gone. His favorite pen, a gift from Grace that also happened to contain a voice recorder for his notes. Gone.

Nothing to see. And yet Erasmus lingered. Something was nagging at him. McIntyre had most likely been working at the couch. He'd slipped off his shoes to get comfortable, loosened his tie. The waiter had come in with the tray. Perhaps McIntyre had not even looked up. And when his guard was down—maybe when he was signing the bill—the waiter had struck.

McIntyre had been standing. Erasmus could tell this by the position of the body. He'd fallen back on the couch. Maybe he'd had only seconds. One arm held close to his body, one arm flopped off the couch and resting, oddly, in his shoe.

Erasmus crossed the room. He squatted by the shoe. He knew he wasn't supposed to touch anything. He had great respect for the Italian police. He didn't want to interfere with their investigation. But the hand on the shoe. The fingers were balled into a fist, except for the index finger. As though McIntyre were *pointing.*

Gently, Erasmus pulled the shoe toward him. He reached inside and felt the crackle of paper. He slipped it out.

For a long moment he couldn't make sense of it, because it made no sense.

A list of cities. Then, just notes, random ones, written in pencil. He saw the words *Guardians* and *Pompeii*.

Noise in the hallway. Time to go.

He placed the paper in the hidden pocket inside his motorcycle jacket. He stood quickly, ready to go. His gaze rested on McIntyre.

No, no . . . this is not the time for grief!

He pushed the swell of emotion back, slipped on his tinted glasses.

"Good-bye, old friend," he murmured. "Rest in peace." His voice broke, and he let the tears fall at last.

Dan sank back down on the cobblestones, his head between his knees. He hadn't told Amy the truth. He was more than shaken up. His head hurt badly.

He could hear Amy's voice explaining, talking, promising Jake that they would find Atticus, that she'd die before she let anything happen to him. Jake looked as though he'd been struck and was about to fall down.

The light was slowly coming up, the blacks smudging to grays. They would get the call, or the text, and it would tell them of another death.

Atticus.

Vesper One had been right here. He had taken the

map and *Il Milione*. If Dan had turned, he could have seen him.

The serum was the only thing that could help him now. The only thing that could fight this was power. More power than the world had ever known.

He felt his phone vibrate in his pocket. He didn't want to see the questions from Attleboro on that phone. He didn't want to give the answers.

He slipped it out of his pocket. The number was blocked.

Suspend judgment. The whole story is always more complex than its parts. Wait. AJT

Dan almost dropped the phone. He read the message again. He reached out and touched the letters *AJT*.

Arthur Josiah Trent.

What he had hoped for as long as he had a memory had happened. He'd gotten a sign.

His father was still alive.

HELLO, CAHILL FRIENDS,

What good little criminals
you are! Up for another caper?
I need a stale orb. Yes, you
read that right—a stale orb.
Can't figure out what that
means? Sadly, it's not my
problem. Just put what I want
directly into my happy hands.
Seven of your relatives are
enjoying my hospitality, and
it won't be pretty if I get sad.

Vesper One